M000166990

THE WORLD'S FINEST ASSASSIN

Gets Reincarnated in Another World as an Aristocrat

Contents

The World's Finest Assassin
Gets Reincarnated in Another World as an Aristocrat

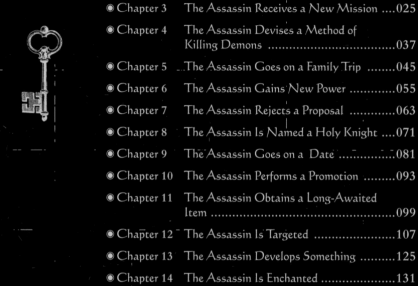

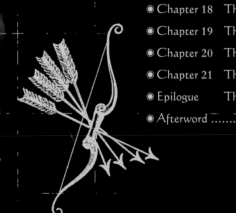

† **Dia**
Despite being older than Lugh, she wound up becoming his little sister. She is among the strongest mages in the world.

† **Maha**
The proxy representative of Lugh's cosmetics brand. She provides logistical support by collecting funds, information, and more.

† **Naoise**
The oldest son of House Gephis, one of the four major dukedoms. He is a handsome boy brimming with talent and has a penchant for hard work.

† **Epona**
The hero. The strongest person in the land, but suffers from anxiety and a lack of self-confidence.

"Lord Lugh's gun protected me... Just one more left!"

"Is that the best they can do? Their mage is nothing special."

† Tarte

Lugh's personal retainer and his assassination assistant. She cares deeply for Lugh because he saved her life.

† Lugh

The oldest son of the clan of assassins, who is often called a boy genius. He was the world's greatest assassin in his previous life, and he combines that knowledge with the magic of his new world.

THE WORLD'S FINEST ASSASSIN

Gets Reincarnated in Another World as an Aristocrat

3

Rui Tsukiyo

Illustration by Reia

YEN ON

New York

The World's Finest Assassin Gets Reincarnated in Another World as an Aristocrat, Vol. 3
Rui Tsukiyo

Translation by Luke Hutton
Cover art by Reia

SEKAI SAIKO NO ANSATSUSHA, ISEKAI KIZOKU NI TENSEI SURU Vol. 3
©Rui Tsukiyo, Reia 2019
First published in Japan in 2019 by KADOKAWA CORPORATION, Tokyo.
English translation rights arranged with KADOKAWA CORPORATION, Tokyo through TUTTLE-MORI AGENCY, INC., Tokyo.

English translation © 2021 by Yen Press, LLC

Yen On
150 West 30th Street, 19th Floor
New York, NY 10001

Visit us at yenpress.com
facebook.com/yenpress
twitter.com/yenpress
yenpress.tumblr.com
instagram.com/yenpress

First Yen On Edition: September 2021

Yen On is an imprint of Yen Press, LLC.
The Yen On name and logo are trademarks of Yen Press, LLC.

Library of Congress Cataloging-in-Publication Data
Names: Tsukiyo, Rui, author. | Reia, 1990– illustrator.
Title: The world's finest assassin gets reincarnated in another world / Rui Tsukiyo ; illustration by Reia.
Other titles: Sekai saikou no ansatsusha, isekai kizoku ni tensei suru. English
Description: First Yen On edition. | New York : Yen On, 2020–
Identifiers: LCCN 2020043584 | ISBN 9781975312411 (v. 1 ; trade paperback) |
ISBN 9781975312435 (v. 2 ; trade paperback) | ISBN 9781975333355 (v. 3 ; trade paperback)
Subjects: LCSH: Assassins—Fiction. | GSAFD: Fantasy fiction.
Classification: LCC PL876.S858 S4513 2020 | DDC 895.6/36—dc23
LC record available at https://lccn.loc.gov/2020043584

ISBNs: 978-1-9753-3335-5 (paperback)
       978-1-9753-3336-2 (ebook)

10 9 8 7 6 5 4 3 2 1

LSC-C

Printed in the United States of America

Prologue | The Assassin Returns Home

Recent events left the academy temporarily closed, and Dia, Tarte, and I were returning to Tuatha Dé.

The demon orc attack a few days ago had destroyed the academy's bulwark, rendering the structure useless as a stronghold and necessitating immediate repair. Many parents were in an uproar, as no one wanted to leave their child at the school when it was in such a state.

Nobles had a duty to fight monsters, and while there was a risk that another force could strike while the academy was out of commission, it didn't make sense to force kids to live in a death trap. Thus, it was decided that students would be sent home until the bulwark was repaired. Functionally, this meant our two-month summer break was starting early.

"There really is no place like Tuatha Dé," Tarte remarked.

"For sure. The artistic and well-organized streets of the royal capital have their appeal, but I prefer Tuatha Dé and its coexistence with nature," I responded.

As had been the case for a while now, the land was covered in soybean fields. The crop was vital in the production of moisturizer, a popular product. For that reason, soybean cultivation was rapidly growing.

Maha's regular reports suggested that Natural You's sales were doing as well as ever. Monsters had started to appear, but profits hadn't gone down because no city had suffered serious damage yet.

However, there was no telling what could happen in the future. One stronghold had already fallen. If the increase in monsters caused a disturbance in the transportation networks between cities, the economy would tank, and demand for luxury items would go down.

According to market research, prices for medicine and weapons were already climbing. Natural You would need to adapt. I wished to meet with Maha in person at least once to discuss this. We needed to form a plan of action soon.

"You look lost in thought again. You're always so busy, Lugh," remarked Dia.

"You're right about that. But that hard work has paid off in spades," I said.

Thanks to my status as a noble, my strength as a Tuatha Dé assassin, and my access to funds and information from the Balor Company, I could have Dia and Tarte at my side and live a life with no restrictions. When I considered that the reward for my work, it didn't seem so bad.

"You toil so much for the sake of others. Personally, I'm most at ease when I'm giving my all to ensure that I myself am happy," Dia stated.

"Lord Lugh seems like he would be able to handle as many wives as he wants…," added Tarte.

"He can't help but come to the aid of every girl in need he finds. Now that I think about it, he really could amass a sizable number of spouses."

"He really could."

"Just who do you two think I am?"

I couldn't deny that I went all out to save Tarte, Maha, and Dia. But I wasn't planning on helping anyone else and luring them into becoming my companion as I had done with those three.

There were things even I couldn't do alone, and that necessitated a team. More people did not necessarily make that team function better. With more members, there came more noise, and reaching mutual understandings would grow more difficult.

Dia and Tarte were my assistants, and Maha provided support. That's all I needed.

"Okay, I trust you... I'm okay with Tarte and that other girl you introduced to me recently, but if you reach out to any more girls, I'll be upset," Dia confessed.

"Ah, um, Maha and I don't really have that kind of relationship with Lugh...," protested Tarte.

"But you want to be that way with him, right?" Dia questioned.

Tarte's eyes darted to my face and away again.

"W–well, yeah, but..."

"Then you should go for it. Like I just said, I won't get mad if it's you."

Why is Dia actively encouraging me to cheat on her? I have no intention of being with anyone other than her.

Perhaps life as a noble had conditioned her to think that way. Continuing the lineage was more important than anything for one of high standing. Military strength was also directly related to the number of mages in the country. For that reason, it was an aristocrat's duty to take multiple wives.

Siring offspring was so crucial that high-ranking nobles with difficulty producing children occasionally paid lower-ranking members of the gentry for reproductive assistance. Tarte didn't have a good understanding of that, so she was blushing and averting her gaze from me.

I'll take Tarte as my second wife.

Should I wind up in a situation where I required a second wife, Tarte could actually work nicely. Being wed to her would allow me to skirt around a few obnoxious hang-ups that came with marrying a noblewoman. Plus, I did take personality and compatibility into account. Regardless, it was too early to be thinking about matrimony.

"That kind of talk would be better saved for after we graduate, wouldn't it?" I asked.

"Yeah, that's true."

"Wha—? Me, marry Lugh…? I, ummm…"

We continued chatting to pass the time and eventually arrived at the estate. I took Tarte's hand, prompting her to blush more intensely than she already was, and led her out of the carriage.

I opened the door to the estate and was immediately tackled by a silver-haired woman.

"Welcome home, my little Lugh! I was so worried when I heard about the demon. Thank goodness you're safe."

"Hey, Mom. There was a demon, but I didn't do anything dangerous. The hero took care of it for us in no time."

"Stop lying! I know what you did. They said you crossed deep into enemy territory alone and alerted the academy to the demon's location."

That was one thing I hadn't concealed in my report to the academy. Evidently, my family had found out.

Epona was first among those credited for repelling the demon attack, but I was second. If we hadn't been able to find the demon, those defending the academy would have fallen from exhaustion. I received great praise for infiltrating the horde of monsters alone, finding the demon, sending up the signal flare to alert the hero to its location, and monitoring the demon until she arrived. Even at that prestigious academy, the number of people capable of such a feat was severely limited.

"We got a letter saying you are going to receive a medal at the royal capital," my mother informed me.

"That's going overboard."

I'd heard from the headmaster that my efforts were greatly appreciated, but there'd been no word of anything like this.

"Oh, come on. You and Cian are the only two in the world who would make that face at receiving an award. You're becoming more and more like him every day."

The Tuatha Dé family lived in the shadows and preferred to stay out of the spotlight. I wouldn't have gone to such great lengths to defeat the demon had it not been necessary. More than anything, drawing attention went against my nature. My dad was of a similar mind.

As if ecstatic over realizing that I was growing similar to my dad, my mom hugged me tighter and pressed my head into her chest. Her breasts were small, so this wasn't incredibly comfortable.

She and Dia really did look alike. Their shared features must have run in the Viekone family.

My mom looked unbelievably young for her age. Dia, my

fiancée, was similarly youthful and slim. I was confident she'd always stay that way, no matter how much time passed. However, that also meant her chest would remain underdeveloped.

"Hey, what's with the weird look?" Dia suddenly inquired.

"I don't know what you mean," I answered.

Dia could be really perceptive at times.

The door then opened again.

"So you've returned, Lugh."

Dad strode into the room. It looked like he was in work mode.

"Yeah, we just got back," I said.

My mom released me, mumbling something and glancing at me reproachfully.

Most of the time, she wouldn't let me go simply because my dad walked into the room, but she never interfered when he was acting as the head of the Tuatha Dé clan of assassins. While a very lovely and free-spirited woman, she was still a member of this family.

"First, allow me to praise you for a job well done. You did very well at getting close to the hero and gaining his trust. It seems like you did brilliantly in your first battle with a demon as well," my dad remarked.

"Apologies for my recklessness," I responded, bowing my head in remorse for standing out more than was necessary.

"No, it's fine. The circumstances have changed. This actually works to our benefit."

Under what circumstances would it be okay for our secretive clan of assassins to stand out?

"That battle was the first skirmish between humans and demons—the opening act of a long fight. For that reason, the Alvanian Kingdom wants to play up victory to raise morale.

Everyone expected the hero to give the performance he did, so his triumph lacked impact. That's why they plan to celebrate your accomplishments. The conferment of a medal has a lot of weight behind it. Make sure you behave in a fitting manner."

"Understood."

A stronghold of young nobles from all over the country falling after the appearance of a single demon could be seen as a demoralizing defeat. The royal family wanted to ensure the populace didn't think that, and the only way to do that was to commemorate what Epona and I had accomplished.

This came as a surprise to me. At least, partially.

"Once you reach the royal capital and receive your honors, many nobles will wish to curry your favor. Make sure not to let them take advantage of you," my dad advised.

"I'll be careful."

"Those are the only matters I had to discuss."

My dad took in a large breath. His demeanor then transitioned from the head of the Tuatha Dé clan of assassins to that of a doting parent.

"…It's nice to have you back. Esri has prepared a feast. I want to hear all about your time at the academy."

"Hmm-hmm-hmm. I made all of your favorites, Lugh. I even prepared some special roast duck and baked my first berry pie in a while."

"That sounds exciting. Dia, Tarte, let's save today's training for after we eat," I said.

"Yes, my lord," Tarte replied.

"Oh, come on, Lugh. Let's just take today off. If we're going to train after we eat, then I can't drink any alcohol," Dia objected.

The pair were clearly excited about the meal. Many strange things were afoot in the world outside, but for now, I was going to enjoy the warmth of home. Having fun and clearing the exhaustion from your mind were important. I'd learned that in this world.

Chapter 1 | The Assassin Goes Hunting

Being home again was a great time. I was blessed with a marvelous family.

Dinner was relaxing. My mom wasn't a gourmet chef, but her cooking suited my tastes. I probably liked it because that's what I grew up on, but my affection for her played a part as well.

The next day, I went hunting in the mountains. I'd decided I would do the cooking today, though not necessarily as thanks for being treated yesterday. Dia wanted to eat my cream stew with rabbit, so I had to go out and gather ingredients.

Turning to Tarte, I inquired, "Are your mana and stamina still okay?"

"Yes, I am managing!" she answered.

My preferred hunting ground was located beyond a deep forest trail and was home to many fierce beasts, which made it quite dangerous. Those areas touched by man had been made easier to traverse, but even walking through the wilderness proved trying on one's endurance. If you weren't careful, your legs could end up scratched, too.

I sought game here to avoid poaching it from commoners. Many made their living from selling meat and skins, and I didn't want to get in their way.

There were many other merits as well. Not even professional

trappers ventured this deep into the wilds, so the area was abundant with fauna. Unworked land like this also made for a good training ground. Hunting here had honed my skills.

"I found Alvanian rabbit tracks... That means it probably hasn't gone far, my lord," Tarte observed.

Traveling through the dense woods tested my agility and stamina, and straining to make sure I didn't miss even the smallest animal traces trained my attentiveness and concentration. It almost felt nostalgic.

Tarte was following behind me. Using only the tiniest trace of footprints left behind, she guessed our quarry's location and took off in pursuit.

I'd given her two assignments during this hunting trip to help her overcome her weaknesses.

The first was to use her Tuatha Dé eyes the entire time she was on the mountain. The Tuatha Dé eyes constantly consumed mana. Without the Rapid Recovery skill, they could quickly cause you to faint. For that reason, a user had to practice maintaining a low mana output. This improved their control over the eyes.

Tarte's other task was to use a new weapon I'd prepared for her. The spear was Tarte's preferred tool in combat. Obviously, she should continue to practice with it and strive to be the best she could. However, I'd given her another armament to use, as well as a shortcut for raising her battle prowess. While it strayed from the honorable combat of knights or martial artists, I didn't care. We were assassins. The pursuit of power was all that mattered.

Tarte took off running while chanting the incantation Dia had made at her request. It was a spell fit for assassination.

"*Wind Shadow!*"

Tarte was very proficient with a spell that created an

aerodynamic wind barrier that removed air resistance, repressed stamina consumption, and enabled her to move at high speeds. This new magic she was utilizing had been based on that. Conjured air gathered around the young woman, boosting her swiftness, disguising her scent, and muffling her sound. As a veritable ghost, she approached the rabbit without fear of detection.

Admittedly, the spell didn't erase all traces of Tarte. That required extremely delicate control, which in turn meant a more difficult incantation. However, those imperfections could be compensated for with assassination techniques, so we didn't worry about it. Achieving all that was easier said than done, though.

"She's doing well," I commented.

Alvanian rabbits possessed acute hearing and smell. Should Tarte approach without being noticed, I'd give her a passing grade.

I was watching this play out from a distance. Tarte lifted her skirt. While she always kept a folding spear on her left thigh, she now sported a handgun with an attachable barrel on her right. That was the new weapon I had gifted her.

"A Gun Strike that Tarte can use. I hope it works," I muttered.

The Gun Strike that Dia and I performed had a few significant shortcomings. It required an explosion of fire magic, which only a select few mages had. While anyone could use Gun Strike if Fahr Stone blasts were employed as a propellant, it required a larger firearm that could withstand the force.

That was why I developed the Fahr Stone powder. By adjusting its quantity, I could regulate the explosion, tapering it as necessary. The bullets in Tarte's gun were filled with the maximum amount of powder a handgun could endure.

Tarte drew the pistol off her right thigh and fitted the attachable barrel to it. A handgun's small size made it easy to use at point-blank range, and affixing the longer barrel raised accuracy for distance shooting.

In less than a moment, Tarte filled the Fahr Stone powder with mana to its critical point. An explosion sounded, and a bullet lanced forth from the handgun, piercing the Alvanian rabbit's head.

Tarte fired the gun with one hand, a feat she was only capable of because she had magically boosted her physical strength. These firearms had twice the kick that a Magnum did. It was enough to knock back even the burliest of men. I'd given the weapon such ridiculous strength because it was intended to kill mages.

"Lord Lugh, I did it! I left plenty for us to eat," Tarte said cheerily.

This was actually the second rabbit she'd shot today. She had struck the first in the middle of its body, ruining the meat. To ensure this didn't happen, you needed to approach it as close as possible, remain calm, and fire a clean shot into the head.

Those were the skills I wanted Tarte to build, and she had succeeded.

"Great job. You've passed. How does the gun feel?"

"I love it. Being able to fire six bullets in a row is amazing."

Tarte cocked the hammer, and the cylinder rotated and loaded the next round.

I'd given her a revolver that held six shots. A semiautomatic pistol would have been better performance-wise. However, it came with a risk of accidental discharge, which I thought was unacceptable. A revolver was better suited to the mechanism that blocked mana from flowing into anything other than the loaded bullet.

"I see. Please let me know if you have any concerns. It's still a prototype, so it needs improvement," I stated.

"Okay! I'll give a detailed report of anything that comes to mind. Test model or not, having powerful magic that doesn't require an incantation is incredible. Any mage could use this."

Just as Tarte said, I'd developed the weapon to be accessible to all. If I ever found highly efficient gunpowder in this world, that would remove the dependency on Fahr Stones, and I would be able to manufacture a firearm that anyone could use, mage or not.

"The era of having to entrust everything to one hero will end someday. This gun could be the first step toward that," I commented offhandedly.

Firearms had brought an end to the knights of medieval Europe. Such fighters were granted privileged lives because they trained from a young age, learned how to use a sword, and ruled over and protected peasants with their superior strength.

Everything changed the moment guns were invented, however. Now, anyone could kill with ease. Years of practice with swords and lances meant nothing in the face of a lead bullet. With only a few days of training, commoners could slay experienced soldiers. Once knights were no longer needed, peasants began to feel exploited, and knights never held the same position in society again.

"Lord Lugh, are you planning on distributing guns throughout the world to bring an end to the current society?" Tarte questioned.

"No, I'm not preparing for anything like that at the moment."

In this world—or rather, in this country—the society of nobles was just barely keeping the peace. I didn't want to do anything to light the embers of war.

"Let's head back."

"Yes, my lord! I'm looking forward to your cream stew. I have never managed to get mine to taste like yours, even though you taught me the recipe. It always feels like something is missing."

I'd first made cream stew here when I was very young, and it became a local specialty of the Tuatha Dé domain. It was served to travelers at inns, and those sightseers spread it throughout the world. Some came to like it so much that they wanted to go to Tuatha Dé just to experience the dish where it originated.

"I really don't do anything special when I make it, though," I admitted.

"Please let me watch you as you cook. That way, I can discover your secret!" Tarte was getting fired up. She did like cooking more than killing.

We entertained idle conversation as we skinned the rabbit, drained it of blood, and wrapped it in tree bark. Once we were back home, I headed for the kitchen right away. Tarte had worked hard hunting today, so I made sure to give her the leg meat, which was the tastiest part.

For dinner, we enjoyed the cream stew with rabbit, some fresh bread, and one more item that I hastily threw together.

I prepared the broth using rabbit bones, dried mushrooms that grew in the mountains, and white sauce. I filled the soup with a typical assortment of seasonal vegetables and rabbit meat.

"My little Lugh's cream stew is truly a masterpiece. There's nothing like a son's home cooking."

"Mom, I often hear 'mother's home cooking,' but I've never heard anyone say 'son's home cooking.'"

"But that's the only way I can describe the flavor. You sure know how to please a woman, Lugh," my mom said with a sigh of pleasure.

"Watch your phrasing," I shot back.

She brought a spoonful of stew to her mouth and smiled from ear to ear.

"Awww, I at least want to surpass Lord Lugh at cooking... I'm a failure as his personal retainer." Looking conflicted, Tarte bit into the leg meat. Its tenderness and flavor made it the tastiest part of the rabbit. Partaking of it was the privilege of the person who'd killed the animal.

Unless we were at the academy, Tarte usually stationed herself behind me as my maid at meals. Today, though, my mom gave her strict orders to eat with us. I wasn't exactly sure what happened, but yesterday, my mom had summoned Tarte for a lengthy discussion. Her eating with us probably had something to do with that. My dad was absent due to something related to my medal ceremony, which presented my mom with the perfect opportunity to get into some mischief.

"This is nostalgic. You made cream stew for me back when I was your mentor, remember? I couldn't believe you created such a delicious meal at such a young age. You've been remarkable ever since you were small, Lugh," Dia said.

"I was just an early developer. I made the gratin you requested, by the way."

"Yes! That's my favorite."

Typically, I prepared gratin the next day using leftovers. However, Dia really wanted some today, so I obliged. All I had to do was coat pasta with cream stew, tomato sauce, and cheese, then bake it—a relatively simple effort.

"Adding rich cheese and the sour taste of tomatoes to the

already delicious cream stew makes it even better," Dia remarked, ecstatically savoring one of her most beloved foods.

Tarte was similarly enjoying the meal, so I offered her some gratin as well. Then I noticed Mom's reproachful glare and gave some to her, too.

That left me without any, but I didn't mind. I made gratin to add a bit of a different flavor to the leftover cream stew the next day. Yet, even so, the taste was still similar. Simultaneously eating both was a little too much for me. I couldn't believe what short work the ladies of the family were making of it.

"That was incredible," my mom said.

"I will take care of cleaning, my lord," offered Tarte.

"I'm going back to my room. Come by later, Lugh. I've finished analyzing the spell you asked me to look at," Dia invited.

The three of them went their separate ways. I decided to head to my chamber to do some work. Although I was curious about what Dia mentioned, I also wanted to improve my prototype gun.

Tarte had been continuously stealing glances at me from the corner of her eye. It was typical behavior whenever she was hiding something from me. She'd done the same thing before giving me a surprise birthday present.

For the time being, I was content to pretend I hadn't noticed. I was worried about whatever nonsense my mom had filled her head with, but I was sure Tarte wouldn't do anything to cause me stress.

Chapter 2 | The Assassin Scolds His Student

I took a moment to stretch. I'd been doing precision work in my room since dinner, so my shoulders were tight.

After seeing Tarte use the gun today, I'd decided on a few minor tweaks. I was satisfied with the force and precision but thought the reloading system could stand to improve.

The two big disadvantages of the mana-blocking mechanism and the size of the gun were the limit of six bullets and the need to restock them all individually after exhausting them. The mana-blocking mechanism, which prevented accidental explosions, also slowed reloading time, and it demanded more effort than a regular revolver.

As the gun was, reloading it in the middle of combat was not realistic. Unfortunately, if I made it easier to load rounds, the mana-blocking mechanism would become less reliable.

"...Maybe I should come at this from a different angle."

I considered the idea of swapping out preloaded cylinders. That sort of thing was common for automatic handguns, but it wasn't impossible for a revolver.

"This should work."

With this new remodel, reloading in the heat of battle was now a possibility. It didn't look like strength would be a problem, either, but spare cylinders were bulky.

"All right, next, I'll make guns for Dia and me."

While Dia and I could both use Gun Strike, employing a gun prepared beforehand would be significantly swifter. Being able to release a lethal attack without the need for an incantation was a huge advantage. Seeing as the weapon was the size of an ordinary handgun, it would be easy to carry as well.

I'd need to reduce the force of Dia's gun, though, as she couldn't match Tarte's physical strength, even after empowering herself with mana.

After calculating the force of the weapon, I drew up a blueprint. The reduced strength meant Dia's firearm could be made smaller. She would have an easier time both carrying it and firing it.

Time flew by as I worked on the design.

"That should do it."

It was getting late, so I decided to end things now that I had completed the design. The building phase would come tomorrow. I crashed onto my bed, and just when my consciousness began to drift away, I heard a knock at the door.

"Lord Lugh, do you have a moment?"

It was Tarte. What could she want at this hour?

"Come in."

I quickly put away all the dangerous stuff I had lying around and then beckoned her in.

"Sorry for coming by so late."

She seemed nervous for some reason, and her voice was trembling. The sight of what she was wearing nearly made me cry out in shock.

"Tarte, what in the world are you doing wearing that?"

"U-um, you know..."

Tarte was dressed only in a white negligee. It clung tightly to her body, and her well-developed arms and legs were bare. The dress was slightly transparent, enough so I could see she wasn't wearing underwear. Her body was also a little flushed, as if she'd come from a hot bath. She looked unbelievably attractive.

A pleasant scent wafted on the air. I recognized the smell from a new Natural You perfume that I developed. We'd added it to meet a demand from customers who wanted something that would entice men.

The product was only distributed in regular shipments to our members. That could only mean that my mom was behind this. She was in regular contact with Maha and had secretly become a member of Natural You.

I'd also laid eyes on the negligee that Tarte was wearing before. My mom showed it off a long time ago while saying something like she would bewitch Dad and give me a little sister. She'd since retailored it for Tarte.

"I can guess most of it already, but I'll ask anyway. Just what did my mom fill your head with?"

"Um, I—I am your assistant, my lord, and an assassin. She said that because girls aren't as strong as boys, they need to compensate by using their bodies as weapons of seduction, so she told me to get some training from you. She also made it clear that as your personal retainer, it's my duty to service you… As an assassin and a maid, I need to, um, do it with you." Red as a beet, Tarte falteringly recounted everything she'd heard from my mom.

In her own way, my mom was likely trying to help, but this was the last thing I needed her doing for me. She was probably only doing it in pursuit of some selfish desire, like wanting to see

the faces of her grandchildren as soon as possible. Tarte had just been unfortunate enough to get swept up in it all.

"Tarte."

I called her name, then grabbed her arms forcefully, threw her onto my bed, pinned her down, and hung over her.

"Eek, Lord Lugh!" she shrieked. Though quivering, her eyes still seemed somewhat impassioned as she looked up at me. Even Tarte's breath seemed sweet. I felt my pulse quicken.

Beholding her in that moment, I wanted desperately to give in to desire. I hadn't considered Tarte as a romantic interest, but this forced me to realize how attractive she was.

Evidently, I still had a lot of maturing to do. My body might have been overflowing with sexual desire, but losing my presence of mind so easily was unbecoming.

Lust wasn't the only thing I was feeling. I was also rather angry at Tarte. I'd have to give her a strict scolding.

"You have no idea what you're saying."

Tarte was ridiculously beautiful. Sexy, too. Even nobles who saw a plethora of enticing women in their lives would want her. She'd drawn the eyes of many at the academy. Some idiots had even approached me about buying her.

"M-my lord, your face is scaring me."

My unusual behavior was causing Tarte to panic. I squeezed her breasts.

"That hurts…"

They were big and soft, and they still had plenty of growing left to do.

"If you're serious about this, I can teach you how to use your body as a tool for assassination. However, you'll have to lie with many people. Do you understand what that means?"

Tarte went silent. My mom had put her up to this, so she hadn't realized what she was committing to. She was only thinking about having sex with me and hadn't thought about what would happen once she finished her training and had to take on a real job.

"Try to imagine it, okay? Using your feminine charms as a weapon means having your body violated by men you don't even like and then looking for an opportunity to kill them."

I put my legs between her thighs to prevent her from closing her crotch. Then I squeezed her breasts even harder.

Tears started to form in Tarte's eyes, and she cowered despite knowing that it was only me.

"You're scared, right? Even with someone you know, you're frightened. I haven't done anything yet, and you're already trembling. Do you really think you can assassinate like this? All right, let's practice. Try it. I'm going to do terrible things to you. Look for an opportunity and shove your gun against my stomach."

I'd instructed Tarte to carry a gun with her everywhere she went. She had one strapped to her even now.

Were this an actual situation, her carrying a firearm in such a way wouldn't be an issue. The holster bound to her thigh wasn't large, and this world wasn't well acquainted with pistols. Her target would believe it to be an accessory of some sort.

I tried to force off Tarte's negligee as tears streamed down her face, and then she pulled the handgun from her holster and aimed for my stomach. She was too slow, however, and I grabbed her hands and twisted.

"That's a failure. This isn't the right moment to strike against a man. If you're going to make a move, it's got to be later, when he's less wary. Wait until he is drunk on lust for you and loses sight of all other things around him."

"I-I'm sorry—"

I let Tarte go and stood up.

"You're not ready for seduction."

I grabbed some tea leaves and cups I had stocked in my room, used a spell to produce some hot water, then brewed Tarte a bit of relaxing tea and handed it to her. She drank it slowly, and she steadily calmed down.

"I had no idea that was going to be so scary. But, um…"

"Are you saying you just weren't ready? Do you want to try again after you prepare yourself?"

"If it will be of help to you," Tarte insisted, locking her still-moist eyes with mine.

Her persistence wasn't because my punishment hadn't been strong enough. This girl was truly determined to do anything for me.

"You're stubborn in the weirdest places. I believe you, but I still won't allow it," I said.

"Because I'm ill-suited for it?"

"No. You are beautiful and have a personality that men love—you're extremely well suited for that sort of job. Your timid nature might work against you, but that could be treated with experience."

Tarte was a hard worker. If she set her mind to a task, she could do it.

"Then why?" she pressed.

"Because the idea of you with another man upsets me," I admitted, speaking from the heart. Tarte was my assistant, but I also thought of her as an important family member.

"What do you mean?"

"Just what I said."

"U-um, I'm happy. I'm happy that I'm dear to you, my lord."

"You always have been. I'm sorry I haven't made that clear."

"That's not what I meant! I know you value me very, very much. That is why I love you, my lord!"

Both of us had been through a lot tonight, and we were confessing things we usually would have kept bottled up.

"After you finish that drink, return to your room and rest. Sorry for scaring you like that," I said.

"It's all right. I understand that it was for my sake. I'm not scared at all anymore."

Tarte was relaxedly sipping her tea. There was no more need for me to fret.

"Um, I won't bring up using seduction for assassination anymore... But, you know, what about my service as a maid?" Tarte asked, looking at me with upturned eyes.

"Let's save that for another day. I don't feel like sleeping with a girl who started shaking just because a man threw her down on the bed."

"Hmph, you're such a bully sometimes, my lord," Tarte pouted.

She then left my room looking happy but also somehow disappointed. When she was gone, I let out a big sigh.

"That was a close call."

Everything I did to Tarte was an act to deter her, but resisting had been difficult. Losing myself and simply making love to her had been very tempting.

"...I'll make Mom pay for convincing Tarte to do something like that."

That was in horrible taste. I overlooked most of her pranks, but this was too much. She needed to be punished.

Chapter 3 | The Assassin Receives a New Mission

The morning after the incident with Tarte, I went to my mom's room.

"Wow! How many years has it been since you've visited my chamber of your own volition, Lugh?! I'll prepare us some tea and sweets. I have some cookies stashed away for a special occasion."

My mom cheerfully stood on a stool to grab some cookies hidden above a dresser. The packaging design was one you'd often see in the royal capital. Doubtless, the sweets were a souvenir someone had sent her that she'd set aside.

"Mom, you know why I'm here, right?"

"Hmm-hmm-hmm, of course I do. You came to thank me for giving Tarte a little push in the back. Did you two go all the way?"

"No, we didn't. I sent her away."

"What, you refused a girl as beautiful as her?! Ah, it's because you don't know how, right? Don't worry. Your mother will teach you."

"That won't be necessary. Receiving that kind of lesson from a parent leads to serious trauma, you know."

Why was she assuming I was a virgin? I had gained plenty of experience while living in Milteu as Illig Balor of the Balor Company. I couldn't date freely while in the position of Illig Balor, however, and I also would have felt guilty because of Dia, so I'd only had sex at brothels. Let's not forget the encounters from my previous life.

The reason I was upset over this was that when I was young back on Earth, I'd used my body to entice people with that sort of predilection. I'd had many acquaintances who'd done the same. I knew how painful and tragic that kind of thing could be.

"If that's not the reason, then I really don't understand. You both like each other deep down, and yet you refuse to get intimate. It's so irritating, I can't take it. That is why I gave Tarte the little push she needed."

"What the hell were you doing telling Tarte to employ seduction? I won't let her do that kind of thing. Surely you must know what it means for an assassin to get involved in that, Mom? How could you send her down that path? I am furious about this."

If it were for me, Tarte would do it. No matter how painful it was for her, she wouldn't hesitate. That's what scared me so much.

"Oh dear, you're scaring me, Lugh. I didn't mean anything by it. It was only an excuse so that she would tempt you."

I had thought that might be the case, but my mom underestimated Tarte's willingness to rush headlong into everything without regard to her well-being.

"The next time you do this kind of thing, I won't forgive you. I'll never speak to you again," I warned.

"N-no, you can't do that. I'll reflect on what I did, so please forgive me. I wouldn't be able to live anymore if you hated me, Lugh."

Clinging to me tight, my mom started to cry. As always, she looked and acted too young for her age.

As I considered that, I realized I had a slight build and often got mistaken for someone younger, too. That would probably continue to plague me even into my twenties. It worried me how people remarked on my resemblance to my mom. It was fine for girls, but no guy wished to look young forever.

"I'm excusing you this time, but no more. I know how Tarte and the others feel about me. We're just fine without you sticking your nose in our business."

Dia, Tarte, and Maha were all valuable companions. We had our own way of doing things, and I didn't want any outside interference.

"Lugh, that's where you're still a child. You have to know there's no way a girl will show her true feelings to the person she likes," my mom stated with a self-satisfied smile.

Although it was irritating, I knew I couldn't deny that.

"Tarte would have been happy if you had laid your hands on her."

"Have you not learned your lesson, Mom?"

"Yes, I have!" she hurriedly replied with a forced bow.

...*She would've been happy, huh?* If I had simply let events unfold and gently slept with her rather than scaring her, it likely would have pleased her.

Still, it was wrong. Relationships built on excuses were unhealthy. Also, if we were to ever truly become involved, that kind of first experience could be damaging down the line.

"I'm leaving."

"Oh, come on, let's have some sweets."

"I'm busy. I won't be able to focus on my own work once Dad gets home."

"He should be back in two days, right? I'm looking forward to seeing what kind of souvenir he brings for us."

"Would that I shared your excitement. I'm being used as a

figurehead to raise the morale of the country. There's no way this won't be trouble."

Dad had left for a preliminary meeting related to my award ceremony. As the capital was far away, the conference was held in a town that served as the halfway point. There were many political machinations at play, and he was summoned as the head of House Tuatha Dé. It felt strange that I wasn't there. I was the one who would be given the medal, after all.

"There's no need to worry. Cian won't let them hurt you, and if he thinks there's danger, I'm sure he'll have an escape plan ready," my mom said.

Most wouldn't expect such preparation from a noble, but it did sound like my dad.

The Tuatha Dé clan worked for the Alvanian Kingdom, but the family was more important to my dad than any country. Should he ever be faced with a choice between the two, it'd be the latter every time. Even without an aristocratic title, he had the strength necessary to protect us.

"Ah, one more thing. Please bring Maha home next time. We've exchanged many letters, and I can feel in her every word how much she loves you. I need to see what kind of girl she is!"

"...Bye, Mom."

There was no point in saying anything more. Feeling very hopeless, I left the room.

To my surprise, my dad returned home a day earlier than expected. As soon as he saw me, he told me we'd meet in the study after an hour and then retired to his room.

He looked to be his usual self at a glance, but I could tell he was concealing profound fatigue. I didn't think I'd ever seen him that spent. The meeting must have gotten quite heated.

I ordered Tarte to brew some of a special tea blend that I'd created. Natural You had added teas to its inventory lately. This one was a rare variety. Even if only a little, I wanted to cheer my dad up. The brew relieved stress and promoted healthy skin, making it quite popular.

"I need to prepare myself for the worst."

I'd been on edge about this whole medal-awarding business, but my dad's mood confirmed that something serious was going on.

"Excuse me," I said as I entered the study. My dad had changed his clothes, and thankfully, his complexion seemed to have improved. Maybe he'd taken a short nap.

"Please sit."

I did as requested.

"Let's get straight to the point. I want to talk to you about your upcoming ceremony in the royal capital. I think you already know this, but the reason I left the domain was to attend a preliminary gathering related to that." His face was solemn as he spoke. That didn't bode well.

Suddenly, a knock came at the door.

"Who is it?" asked my dad.

"It's Tarte. I brought tea on Lord Lugh's orders."

"Enter."

Tarte bowed and then poured two cups. She'd become quite graceful at this. Once finished, she bowed again and left the room.

"This smells nice. I'm not familiar with this tea," my father remarked.

"It's tea from a distant foreign country. It's supposed to be relaxing," I replied.

"...To think I let my own son see how tired I really was. It won't be long now until you are head of the house. This brew is good. Just what I needed."

Dad drank with a slight smile, and his facial expression softened a little.

The tea was made using mana that leaked from the ground located above flowing dragon veins, making it impossible to find during my first life. I took a great liking to it and ended up buying some fields and tenant farmers from a landowner to secure a private supply. To ensure a good work ethic, I paid the workers much higher salaries than their previous employer.

"Now that we've had time to relax, let's get back to our discussion. The medal ceremony in the royal capital will play out roughly as I expected, so there are no real problems there. You will have to be a part of some overly showy functions, though."

"I'm prepared for that."

My dad filled me in on the details, and nothing seemed particularly off. None of it pushed past what I was comfortable with.

"The real issue is what will follow... This attack has left the leaders of this country shaken. A single demon's appearance led to your school being devastated, despite it possessing the highest concentration of mages anywhere in the nation. To make matters worse, it all happened in the royal capital's backyard."

The Royal Knights Academy was situated on the outskirts of the royal capital.

The capital had two layers of defense—its actual military establishments and the academy.

Many strongholds on the outside had been rendered all but meaningless during the demon incursion, and the school had been moments from falling. We were one mistake away from the royal capital, the pillar of the country, being destroyed.

"If they're scared, then they'll take a defensive strategy... No, they wouldn't... Are they planning on keeping the hero in the capital?"

"Very astute. When the next demon appears, the hero will not be permitted to venture too far from the capital. Our rulers are ready to sit by and let people die. The excuse is that if they fall, then so, too, does the country. Truthfully, those higher up in the government are just looking out for themselves."

They were going to keep the hero locked up in the royal capital even though demons couldn't be killed without her. It was utterly insane.

"What does that have to do with House Tuatha Dé or me?" I asked.

"...The nobles of domains farther from the capital were vehemently against this tactic. None of them liked the idea of being left for dead. That is when your name came up. The central government convinced everyone to accept keeping the hero at the capital by promising to dispatch enough fighting strength to kill a demon, should another make itself known."

"They're going to send me? Why does the capital think I'm capable of that sort of thing?"

I did participate in the last battle, but as far as anyone knew, all I did was discover the demon's location and then keep an eye on it until the hero arrived. None of that was enough for people to think I could battle a demon head-on.

"From what I understand, Epona let a few things slip. You were careless, Lugh," chided my dad.

"...Shoot. I'm sorry."

I'd asked her not to say anything. I knew full well that if my strength ever became known, it would be problematic.

"Don't blame the hero. As I understand it, some folks were badmouthing you at a party, and he spoke out in your defense... You can probably imagine what followed, right?"

"Knowing Epona's personality, yeah. I was too naive."

She most likely revealed everything I did during that battle. Still, I couldn't blame Epona for this. It was my mistake for not binding her with anything more than a verbal promise.

"I don't know if this is something you'll be happy about, but you will receive appropriate compensation for this role. In my efforts to protect you, I demanded ridiculous compensation, hoping it would get the higher-ups to back off, but those fools accepted everything I asked for. And that's not all. It was decided you will be awarded a special position at your medal ceremony. The station will come with a variety of privileges. I apologize for not being able to protect you. Our family has long evaded rising beyond the level of baron because of the freedom that rank affords us, but this whole debacle was a good reminder of how little one is capable of without a superior standing."

Those running the government were as sly as ever.

Dad was unrivaled in matters of assassination and medicine. When it comes to politics, however, a person's standing speaks more than their skill. It was actually impressive he was able to obtain as much as he did.

"Please don't apologize. My own naïveté caused this. It's my price to pay," I said.

"You continue to amaze me, Lugh. If you ever feel the need, you can flee the country. If it's gotten to the point where I have to send my son to certain death, then I won't hesitate to abandon our lives here. All preparations are ready."

My dad was undoubtedly referring to the plan for if House Tuatha Dé was ever cast aside by the royal family. In his eyes, I could see the conviction to betray our nation to save me.

That's the sort of man my dad was. When it came to assassination techniques, even I didn't match him. He was reliable, but that's precisely why I didn't want to grow overly dependent.

"For now, I don't think that's necessary. I'll prove I'm capable of even killing a demon," I declared.

Technically, this was a meteoric rise in standing for me. The reality of the situation, however, was that I was being thrown into a battle against demons without the hero's help. Functionally, it was suicide.

I was sure the government didn't believe I could actually kill a demon. My involvement was just an excuse to keep the hero in the capital. Should I wind up dead, the bigwigs would simply tell the provincial nobility to honor their agreement and continue to hog the hero for themselves.

Regardless, I was already devising a way to slay demons. This new development only meant that I had to speed up my work.

"There is some other business," my dad added. "I was entrusted with a message from Epona. He says he wants to meet with you before the medal ceremony. As a token of apology, the hero wants to use his skill My Loyal Knights to share some of his power with you."

It came as a surprise that Epona had been present at the meeting. Likely, it was so she could provide testimony to my strength.

"That would help a lot. The idea of going up against a demon as I am now has me feeling rather powerless. Leave it to the hero to have a skill that can be shared with others."

Truthfully, I already knew of that ability. It was an S-Rank skill I'd learned about while in the goddess's room.

My Loyal Knights enabled the user to strengthen up to three people and give them copies of the original's skills. However, if one of the targets went against the hero or fell in battle, they'd lose that gift.

That power was something I could make use of to kill the hero. There were plenty of loopholes to get around the condition of not being allowed to oppose Epona.

"Are you really okay with this? I think it would be perfectly acceptable if you run," my dad said again.

"Don't worry. I wouldn't agree to anything I can't do. Assassins don't misjudge themselves. That's how you raised me. I promise I'll be fine. Also, this isn't so different from what we've been doing up until now. The role of the Tuatha Dé is to assassinate those who will bring harm to our country. All that's changed is the opponent."

This was shaping up to be a tremendous task, but it could've been worse. My dad explained the special privileges I would be granted, and they were very enticing. Ultimately, my regular practices wouldn't be too heavily altered.

As a Tuatha Dé, I'd do anything for the country. Even assassinate a demon.

Chapter 4 | The Assassin Devises a Method of Killing Demons

In a whirlwind of unexpected developments, I had been saddled with a duty to slay demons and a higher standing in the aristocratic hierarchy.

If I was going to make it to the award ceremony, I had to leave Tuatha Dé in two days. That meant today and tomorrow were the only times I'd have to hunker down and focus on my research.

As I was drinking some tea in my room, there was a knock at the door.

"Lord Lugh, I'm here."

"Why'd you call us so suddenly? Did something happen?"

"I've been waiting on you two."

Dia and Tarte entered. I wanted to speak with them about what my dad had said. The two of them were my assistants. Should I go up against a demon, they'd be right there with me. They needed to be apprised of the situation.

"I have something I need to tell you two. The country has entrusted me with a heavy responsibility."

I recounted everything, and both girls reacted with surprise.

"You never cease to amaze, Lord Lugh. This sounds like a massive promotion! What is that special rank?"

"There's something wrong with the people of this country.

I can't believe they would force a job like killing demons onto a single noble."

Both seemed surprised, though for different reasons. Tarte was overjoyed at the recognition of my strength, while Dia looked on things with a bit more cynicism. I thought the latter was the correct response.

"First of all, is it even possible to kill a demon? Every bit of research suggests that only the hero can do it," Dia said.

"I don't think it is. I fought the demon during the battle at the academy. I was able to slay it, but I couldn't keep it dead. Its might eclipsed mine two- or threefold. I cut that thing down eleven times, and it rose back up in each instance without fail. Only the hero can kill a demon," I replied.

That battle had been frightening. No matter what I did, that creature wouldn't stay down. Changing the methods by which I slew it did reveal a few things, however. But I hadn't been able to make much use of my findings in the thick of the fight.

"Then you can't do it, my lord. It sounds like you have no chance. Demons seem really hard to eliminate," Tarte commented.

"That's true. For now," I said.

"Then you do know of a way of defeating them after all?" questioned Dia.

"That's right. Every time I killed the demon, I analyzed it with my Tuatha Dé eyes from the moment of death to the point it revived. I did the same when Epona slew it. By doing so, I was able to construct a hypothesis on why the task is something only the hero can do."

"Lugh, that's incredible. Every nation in the world has been tirelessly searching for a way to kill demons for years," Dia commented.

Dealing with those creatures had been a problem plaguing the entire world for centuries. They only appeared about once every two hundred years, but they always brought death and destruction with them.

The hero's home country would survive, but everyone else suffered a tragic fate. The hero was only sent to help other nations after they paid an outrageously steep price.

It was such a serious issue that some allied lands had agreements that stipulated shared use of the hero should they be born there.

"I owe my realization to the Tuatha Dé eyes. It was only because I could see mana that I figured it out. No other researcher in the world has had that chance."

Without the vision I possessed, it was impossible to find the solution. Even the act of accompanying the hero onto the battlefield and observing a demon up close wouldn't have been enough. If only one of those many researchers could see mana, they might have found the answers they so desperately sought.

"That's still unbelievable! If your theory proves true, it could change the world," said Dia.

Monopolizing the method of slaying demons didn't seem worthwhile. I was sure the government wouldn't want such information getting out, so that they could use the hero as a bargaining chip with other countries. However, as someone forcibly tasked with killing demons, the more people who could do it themselves, the better.

"That's exactly why I need to focus on getting this done as quickly as I can. Once I do, I'll teach you both," I stated.

"Okay! With you teaching me, I'm sure I'll be able to do it!" Tarte declared.

"I'll help you develop it. I'm sure this method uses magic," Dia added.

"That it does. I'm counting on you two."

It would be a heavy load for me to bear alone. But with Dia and Tarte by my side, I felt like I could pull it off.

"I have a present for both of you as well. Tarte, I remodeled your gun. It now has replaceable chambers that should make loading easier. And Dia, I made you a custom model."

"Truly?! The one you gave me before was already amazing!"

"It's so cute and small. I'll be able to keep this on me at all times."

I passed the girls their revolvers. Dia's was more compact than Tarte's.

Even if Dia were to strengthen herself with mana, she would be unable to handle the recoil of Tarte's gun. For that reason, I made her a less powerful model.

"It's about the size of a hand, so I've dubbed it the handgun. The barrel is short, making it easy to wield and conceal. Unfortunately, the trade-off is that it's less accurate. Tarte has the option of attaching a long barrel. But Dia, if you feel you have the time for long-distance aiming, use Gun Strike."

"I'll practice hard, my lord."

"The rapid-fire mechanism looks complex. Producing this with a single spell seems all but impossible. Your gift is a fantastic boon."

There was a chance the girls could become targets down the line. I thought it best for them to have some manner of self-defense available anywhere.

"That's all I have to say. Tarte, return to your training. Dia and I are going to research how to kill demons," I instructed.

"Understood."

"I'm eager to hear about your hypothesis."

There was no time to waste. We had to find a way to kill demons before more appeared.

"First thing to note is the reason demons can't be killed. Their bodies are false—demons aren't alive in the traditional sense. Each one possesses a core that contains what is their power of existence. Whenever a demon is injured, the core can disassemble the damaged part of the body and use its power to reconstruct it," I explained.

"I have a question. Does that mean if you break the core, the demon will die right away?" Dia asked.

"Only if you can get the core to materialize. The core is some kind of spiritual object or mass of power. There's nothing physical to be touched there."

"Wow, this sounds really difficult."

I'd figured all of that out as I was repeatedly killing the demon that attacked the academy. My Tuatha Dé eyes were able to grasp the existence of the core and the power spilling out of it.

"The reason the hero can kill demons is that they envelop their body with a unique energy. In battle, it spreads to create a field. A demon's core is forced to materialize within that field, losing its ability to deconstruct and restore its body at the same time."

"So it becomes unable to heal injuries, and the core can be broken, right?"

"Correct, which makes killing it simple. We only need to

re-create that force the hero generates. It looked to be formed by taking energy and the natural mana of the world and fusing them with a specific wavelength of physical mana. The hero is naturally able to control the flow of magical power that inhabits the world to obtain an exquisite balance, but we'll have to recreate that with magic."

There were two types of mana. The first was physical mana, which flowed within our bodies. It was also known as odic force. Natural mana was the second. This was the force that enriched the world. It was divided into five different colors: one for each basic element, plus an attributeless version.

"It's important that we get the distribution right. The field will only form when you mix the determined ratio of the five colors of natural mana with the required wavelength of physical mana and then bring them into harmony using energy. The hero can do all of that subconsciously, but it will be challenging for us."

"My head hurts just listening to that. But I think we can do it. There are many spells that use the power of natural mana. If I can find common spots in their formulas, I should be able to deduce how to gather it. Do you know the ratio?"

"Yeah, I saw it during the fight. If we have a spell that can gather the five colors of natural mana, it would be possible to form the wavelength of physical mana we need and combine the two using energy."

"Lugh, you're making that sound easy, but unless forming the wavelength of mana and controlling energy can be done automatically, no one but you will be able to use this spell. Those aren't things normal people are capable of."

"I understand that, but a formula can't automatically control the mana and energy. We'll simply have to practice and master that ourselves. You and Tarte should be able to do it. I'm not so sure about anyone else, though."

"This is going to be very challenging, but let's do it. Success means being able to kill demons."

"That's right. I'm confident this will work. Unfortunately, even if we finish the spell, it will still possess a major flaw."

"What do you mean?"

"Producing a field that forces demons' cores to manifest demands vast amounts of mana. At best, I think I can only barely manage it, even if I push to the absolute limit. The user won't have much mana left for physical strengthening while casting the field."

If I took the drug that removed the limiter on my brain, I'd likely be able to keep fighting, but even then, I'd be battling with a severe handicap.

"Once again, Lugh, only you will be able to use this. If even you can barely manage it with your absurdly high mana capacity, how is anyone else supposed to be able to do it?" Dia questioned.

My quantity of magical power was a little over one thousand times higher than the average mage, and it was still growing. It was the only area where I surpassed the hero. My discharge rate outstripped others tenfold. Yet, for all that, I'd only barely be capable of using this spell. An average mage would have no chance.

"Let's work on finishing this new magic first. We can worry about reducing the amount of power it consumes afterward. Regardless of whether I'm the only one who can use it or not, it will still give us a fighting chance."

Drawbacks aside, this would enable us to kill demons. I could inflict lethal damage by using a low-mana weapon like a gun or an explosive. I could also release Gungnir beforehand and then produce the field the moment it landed. There were many possibilities, including leaving the fighting to Tarte and Dia.

"You're right, Lugh. This will be really tough, but I'm sure we can do it together."

"Yeah, I know we can do it," I replied.

"Also, I have one request." Dia blushed and poked the tips of her index fingers together timidly. "After we finish this spell, take me on a date. We haven't been able to do anything romantic recently. I know you're busy, but I can't help feeling lonely."

Her face broke into a smile. She truly was cute.

"As soon as our work is done, I'll take you out. I promise."

"Okay! No backing out, now."

"Of course. I'm looking forward to it, too."

A date with Dia sounded lovely. It was yet another reason to endeavor hard. Suddenly, I was filled with motivation.

Chapter 5 | The Assassin Goes on a Family Trip

Dia and I were holed up in the workshop for two entire days. We'd been researching passionately nonstop.

"And it's done."

"Whew. I can't believe we've come this far in just two days."

I looked back over the formula for the spell we'd just completed.

We'd spent the last forty-eight hours working on a formula for gathering natural mana at the ideal ratio. Had I done this alone, I guessed it would've taken me half a month. It was because of Dia that we swiftly discovered how the law for gathering natural mana functioned. Although it possessed terrible efficiency, we now had a spell that met the minimum requirements.

"The next part is up to me," I said.

With the spell completed, the only thing left to do was practice. The field would only form if I could successfully gather the five colors of natural mana at the ideal distribution, add the correct wavelength of physical mana, and use energy to combine them. Controlling all of that came down to skill.

"Don't worry. I know you'll be able to do it. The real problem is that we can't actually prove it works. I don't doubt your theory, but we won't know how effective this is without a real demon," Dia remarked.

"You're exactly right."

In the end, all we did was realize a theory based on my recollections of what I'd seen in a battle. We'd only get to test it in actual combat, and failure meant death.

Should it come time to fight a demon and this formula didn't work, we'd have no recourse but to flee. Running hadn't been an option at the academy, but knowing when to escape was a talent like any other.

"Now we can go on our date, like you promised. I'm looking forward to seeing where you'll take me, Lugh." Dia cheerfully wrapped her arm around mine. Her smell and the softness of her skin were making me dizzy. The incident with Tarte a few days ago still had me feeling a little uneasy.

A date, huh? I'm sure I could find time for one when we're away for my award ceremony.

"I guarantee we'll have a great time. I know a decent amount about the royal capital," I replied.

While the academy was in a more suburban area, it was still part of the city. I always thoroughly investigated the places I lived. Knowing how to use the land was vital for an assassin.

Dia rubbed her eyes.

"Are you tired?" I asked.

"A little, yeah."

She'd hardly slept these past two days. Once Dia went into research mode, she forgot all about exhaustion. I had Rapid Recovery, so that wasn't an issue for me, but she needed rest.

"I'll carry you to your room."

"Okay, that would be great."

I picked Dia up in my arms like a princess, and she put her hands around my neck. Then we made for her room.

As was ever the case, her chamber was filled to bursting with various implements and books related to magic and sported no girly affectations whatsoever. I laid her down on the bed.

"We're here, Dia. Can you let go of me?"

Although I wasn't carrying her anymore, she didn't seem at all willing to release me.

"Oh, Lugh, you never take my invitations." Dia sighed, looking up at me with mischievous eyes.

I swallowed hard. "Someday. It's still too soon."

"I'm waiting for you. I'm ready anytime... Doing this is embarrassing, you know. But I'm afraid if I'm too passive, someone else will get to you first."

She really is adorable. Hearing her sound so eager nearly made me lose control.

Early the following day, my dad and I pulled out the horses and the carriage and furnished them with expensive raiment and gaudy bridles that we didn't regularly use.

Receiving a medal in the royal capital demanded a certain level of etiquette. That extended even to the carriage. Arriving in a shabby conveyance would cause people to make fun of House Tuatha Dé and call us country bumpkins, so this preparation was essential.

"This should do," muttered my dad as he completed the flawless decorations.

An assassin needed to be able to deal with any situation. As such, my dad and I could do just about anything. Even the carriage was homemade.

"You've got a talent for this, Dad. If we had a little more time, I would have been able to procure some things from Milteu to make it seriously fancy, though," I stated.

"It's fine as is. We've made it good enough. Anything more would be pointless."

As Dad said, this was just enough for us to avoid scorn. If we went flashier, people might start to think we'd grown full of ourselves despite our lowly station as a baron family. Aristocracy was truly fickle and annoying.

"Cian, Lugh, we're ready, too."

"Wow, I wouldn't have thought the ever-practical House Tuatha Dé would have this kind of carriage."

Mom and Dia walked up to us, their silver hair dancing in the wind behind them. Both were carrying large suitcases that held spare underwear and dresses for parties. I was being recognized for my accomplishments, and as my family, they needed to sport the appropriate attire.

"Wait, Dia, what will you be wearing?" I inquired.

She had come here from the Viekone domain with nothing but the clothes on her back. All the daily necessities were provided for her, of course, but she didn't have any formal gowns for parties in the royal capital.

"I'm wearing some of Esr...er, Mom's old dresses," Dia answered.

"They fit her perfectly. I wanted to have Tarte wear some of them, but they're too tight on her chest," my mom elaborated.

"I'm sure Tarte will be fine in servant clothes," I replied.

Each house was permitted to bring one or two servants to the festivities. There were exceptions, but most of them wore attendant garb instead of formal vestments.

Speaking of Tarte, where is she?

No sooner had the thought crossed my mind than she came running over to us, carrying a large basket.

"I'm sorry I'm late!"

"There's no need to rush. We still have plenty of time before we need to leave," I said.

"That's a relief."

"What's that?"

"I made us all some boxed lunches. I planned to get them finished a little earlier, but this morning, Mr. Hans brought some eggs as a thank-you gift for curing his cow. I thought it would be a waste not to eat them today while they're fresh, so I added them to our meals," Tarte explained.

"Ah, thanks. That was very kind of him," I said in return.

Hans had gone through the trouble of coming by so early because he wanted to give me the eggs at their best. Tarte knew leaving them for after we got back from the royal capital would be putting that goodwill to waste. She had always been the type to show deep consideration for others.

"I'm sure they're very high quality, so I hope everyone's looking forward to eating them. I made the faloodeh you love, Lord Lugh," Tarte added.

"That sounds wonderful. If there's nothing else, then we should be on our way," I declared.

"Yes, my lord," answered Tarte.

The entire family climbed into the carriage, and the horses got moving.

"This is our first family trip in three years. We haven't had any opportunities since you went to Milteu, Lugh," my mom remarked.

"Yeah. The last time was when we went to Margrave Gullanar's party," I replied.

That had certainly been an obnoxious escapade. Margrave Gullanar was a prominent noble who managed the entire region and held political power equal to a duke. From the position of a lowly baron's family, he may as well have been living on the clouds.

Along with all other noble households in the area, my family had been asked to attend his heir's wedding. Despite our usual dogged persistence in avoiding such high-profile social functions, even we hadn't been able to refuse.

"You looked so cute in that outfit I had you wear," my mom said with a sigh as she reminisced.

"...That was traumatic for me."

As per usual, my mom had forced me to don clothes she'd made. While that particular outfit thankfully had pants instead of a skirt, it still looked undeniably feminine. Adults at the wedding had fallen over themselves at how cute I looked, and the kids made fun of me for looking like a girl. It was best not to care what other people thought of you, but I'd wanted nothing more than to melt through the floor back then.

"You've been getting so mean lately, Lugh. I went through all the effort of tailoring your outfit for this ceremony, and you refused to wear it."

"Sorry, Mom, but I've already picked out one I like."

As a young executive of the Balor Company, Illig Balor required regular formal attire, so I had plenty of outfits to choose from. Naturally, the ensemble I selected was one I'd never worn out before, to keep people from suspecting that Illig and I were the same person. Maha had sent it to me in advance because

I'd anticipated that my mom would try to put me in something homemade.

While making conversation with my family, I noticed a presence and gave my dad a sign. The Tuatha Dé clan possesses a technique that allows us to communicate to an extent without using our voices.

Dad, we're being tailed. Two people.

I detected them, too. Judging by their movements, they're here to observe.

Should we go after them? They're decently skilled, but no trouble for us.

Let's leave them be. I don't think they're enemies for now. Likely, they're here to evaluate.

We weren't even at the royal capital yet, and already we had a tail. My award ceremony had saddled House Tuatha Dé with a lot of attention.

Although our work as assassins was kept secret, my family was still famous thanks to its achievements in the medical field. As the Tuatha Dé heir and acting substitute for the hero, I was going to stand out whether I liked it or not.

I could only guess at who these pursuers worked for. My dad and I had decided not to engage them, but if they showed any intention of hostility, I'd exterminate them without holding back.

After a long journey in our horse-drawn carriage, we arrived at the royal capital. On the way, we passed by the academy and saw that the reconstruction was progressing swiftly. From what I could tell, it might reopen sooner than planned.

Some knights from the Royal Alvanian Order came to guide us after we passed through the city gate and announced our identity. We were to head to the palace immediately. Living quarters had been prepared for us.

That was an unexpected revelation. My family and I had intended on staying at one of the city's inns until the day of the award ceremony.

"I can't believe we're going to be staying in a castle. My little Lugh has become such an amazing young man," my mother said with a sigh.

"This is incredible. I'm sure the structure has plenty of rooms for visitors, but a baron's family typically isn't extended this courtesy," I remarked.

"You never cease to impress, my lord... Still, I'm nervous at the idea of staying in a palace," Tarte admitted.

My mom and Dia were in high spirits. The same could not be said of my dad, however, who seemed troubled.

"This is likely an indicator of how much they're expecting from Lugh," he stated.

"We don't know if that's their intention. It might only be a front so that those upset about keeping the hero in the capital don't lose faith in me," I replied.

Our carriage rolled along the city streets and onto the grounds of the alabaster castle. As one would expect of the nation's seat of power, it was an impressive building. High walls and a deep moat encircled it, and countless ballista and mechanisms for pouring molten iron dotted the parapets. Soldiers were stationed in every tower, constantly on the lookout.

Despite such features, it managed to look resplendent. Violence and beauty coexisted in this place. I actually quite liked it.

Beyond the castle gate was an incredible garden that had to be several hundred meters wide. Every flower was in bloom, and the trees were pruned in an artful fashion. Decorative fountains littered the area.

"Wow...it's so pretty. This kind of garden would be impossible even in Viekone," commented Dia.

"I wonder how much money this all costs," I mused idly.

The amount of money spent every month on this garden's upkeep could feed hundreds. That said, this enclosure didn't exist for pleasure alone. It also served as a symbol of the nation's prestige, so I couldn't declare it a total waste.

Our carriage and horses were taken into the care of palace staff, and my family and I were led to our quarters by a group of servants. They asked us to relax until summoned.

The rooms were practically a home unto themselves, with a fully furnished kitchen, a living room, a few bathrooms, and six bedrooms. There was also a simple refrigerator stocked with plenty of water and an impressive collection of foreign fruits. Should we have required anything more, there was a bell to summon servants at any time of day. It was palatial in every sense of the word.

Tarte looked dumbfounded. "All these paintings and vases are amazing."

"If you broke one of those, you'd end up enslaved for life trying to pay it off."

When maids committed careless mistakes, they were occasionally forced to pay with their bodies. However, breaking any of the expensive pieces here earned you a debt even a lifetime working in brothels couldn't pay off.

"Eek!" Tarte moved away from a vase and cowered. I understood the feeling.

We each picked out a room. Trembling, Tarte asked me whether it was appropriate for her to be here, but I assured her that I didn't mind. Depending on the situation, I'd prefer her as my servant to any of the castle staff.

As soon as we changed into the comfortable loungewear provided for us, an attendant arrived. They informed me that Epona had requested my presence.

Evidently, the time had come for Epona to bequeath some of her power to me using her skill My Loyal Knights. I wondered exactly how much she could give me.

Chapter 6 | The Assassin Gains New Power

"Tarte, can you come with me?" I called out as I was getting myself ready.

"Yes, my lord!"

"I'm gonna stay here," said Dia.

I left the room together with Tarte.

The idea that the hero was going to grant me some of her skills seemed too good to be true. Still, I had no reason to refuse. I trusted Epona.

◇

The higher you climbed in this castle, the more opulent the furnishings became. Only the royal family was permitted on the top level, and the one below it was used by those directly beneath the royal family in terms of rank.

Tarte and I were brought to the second-highest floor. As the lowly son of a baron, it was unthinkable to enter such a place. That was just how highly regarded the hero was.

I felt many gazes on me as I walked. These people already recognized what I looked like.

"Did they send around a portrait of me or something?"

While I disguised my face during assassination jobs, I still wasn't happy about all this popularity.

Our destination was a conservatory that protruded from the castle proper. The ceiling and floor were constructed from special glass, making it feel like we were in a floating flowerbed.

Epona was in the middle of the room. As soon as she saw me, she ran up and bowed her head.

"Lugh, I'm so sorry! You told me not to say anything, but I ended up losing my temper and revealing everything. It's because of me that you wound up involved in all of this!" She then proceeded to bend at the waist a few more times.

"Don't worry about it. I don't mind."

"I'm really sorry."

"I'm telling you, it's okay."

I understood that Epona was the sort who would say anything when her emotions got the better of her. Going forward, I would have to be careful not to let slip too much critical information around her.

"Um, well, I know apologizing isn't enough, so I thought I'd use my skill. It's called My Loyal Knights."

Guess we're getting straight to it.

"What kind of skill is it?" I asked knowingly.

"Let's see, I can lend my power to three people throughout my lifetime. I say lend, but that doesn't mean I give away my strength—I still remain the same. To be more specific, you get mana, physical might, and a few of my skills," explained Epona.

"That would be a significant boon. I'm going to be fighting demons, so every little bit will help."

"There are some conditions, though. If you oppose one of my orders, then you will lose the effects of My Loyal Knights, and the same thing will happen if you suffer defeat in a battle with something important at stake. Those conditions still apply even if I were to die. Once a person loses my power, I can't grant it to them again."

Losing this boon if I disobeyed her meant doing whatever she commanded, no matter how impossible. That could be troublesome.

However, the biggest drawback was probably the loss upon being defeated in combat. Once you obtained this skill, you could never lose again.

I hadn't known it had to be a struggle with something precious hanging in the balance, though. If what Epona said was correct, then being bested in training was no problem.

"Have you ever used it on someone?" I inquired.

"I actually have used it once. Shortly after I awoke as the hero, I used it on a huge man with blue hair near the Soigelian border."

Wait. I know someone who fits that description. It couldn't be...

"His power hasn't come back to me yet, so I think he's still doing well," added Epona.

"I'm curious, what skills did you give him?"

"Berserk and some others. I don't think I can choose which ones someone receives from My Loyal Knights. Those that best suit the recipient are chosen."

Did this mean that Setanta, the man I'd fought to protect Dia, got his strength from Epona? He'd mentioned something about never having a real fight before, so he must have been incredibly strong from the get-go. Somewhere along the way, he presumably met Epona and became a monster.

When I faced him, I thought it couldn't have been a

coincidence that he happened to have Berserk and a skill that allowed him to maintain his reason even in that savage state. However, I may have gotten it backward. There was a chance Setanta possessed an ability that kept his mind clear first, and that was the reason My Loyal Knights had given him Berserk.

Epona had unknowingly confirmed something terrible. Her sensing that Setanta was okay meant he had somehow survived our encounter. We'd probably meet again at some point.

He did wager something important during that battle. Does the fact that he didn't forfeit his power mean he's aware that he didn't lose the duel, but was instead caught off guard? If that's the case, then that stipulation seems quite lenient.

"I see. So that's how it works. Are you sure about this, though? You can only use it on three people," I said.

"Yes, it's no problem. You saved me, after all. It's thanks to you that I can be the hero. This will help you keep your promise," replied Epona.

I'd sworn that if she ever became a monster, I'd put her down. That was the very reason I'd been sent to this world.

"Got it. Then I accept your offer," I stated.

"All right, here goes." Wasting no time, Epona placed her hands on my shoulders. They glowed with a faint green light, which sank into my body.

"Okay, it's done. You should be able to use some of my skills now, Lugh."

"Was that really it?"

The entire thing was wholly anticlimactic.

"All I did was use the skill. Next, I'd like to give you this. I had to pull some strings to get it for you." Epona produced an appraisal sheet, a rare item that revealed what skills you had.

I went ahead and used the magical item. The hero had granted me five new skills. Out of those, two caught my eye immediately.

The first was My Loyal Knights. I couldn't believe I had miraculously gained the very skill that bequeathed me this new power in the first place. Regardless, I was grateful for it. I could use it to strengthen Dia and Tarte. They would be joining me in battles against demons, and I had been worried that their standard training would be insufficient.

Possibility Egg was the other big prize. I'd gone back and forth about picking this A-Rank skill a lot before being reincarnated. Based on the owner's nature, it could become any other skill from S Rank to B Rank. Had I used my A-Rank slot on it, there was a chance I could have ended up with another S-Rank skill, but I hadn't thought the gamble was wise at the time. There was a risk it could never become another skill.

The rest of the new abilities were all versatile and mighty, precisely what I'd expect from skills chosen from among the hero's collection.

"What skills did you get?" Epona questioned.

"Surprisingly, I got My Loyal Knights. I wonder if that happened because I have experience teaching a lot of people," I answered.

"I think it's perfect for you... You know, I honestly believe you're capable of killing a demon. But, Lugh, if you prove unable, flee and call for my help. I'll come running even if it means disobeying the king." Epona took my hand in hers as she made her declaration. She must have felt closer to me than I had assumed.

"Should it come to that, I will. But I'll do my best to ensure that won't be necessary. Focus on protecting the country, and I'll do the killing. Those will be our roles."

Hopefully, that would leave Epona less likely to destroy the world. Because the hero thought so highly of me, however, my death could now be the trigger for her going mad. I didn't appreciate that twist of irony.

"Yeah, that sounds good. Let's guard the world together. You're more of a hero than I am, Lugh."

"That's not true. I'm as far from it as you can get."

No matter where life took me, I was an assassin.

Epona released my hand and stood up. "Okay, I'm going to head back. Someone important is expecting me. I think your workload is only going to increase from here, but do your best. Actually, you'll probably fare much better than me. All right, see you."

Once the hero was gone, Tarte, who had been standing behind me the entire time, spoke. "That was quick, my lord."

"Yeah, it was a bit uneventful. But this is even more power than I was expecting."

If this was the secret of Setanta's might, then I at least wanted to match his strength. I hoped to run some tests on these new skills.

"After I experiment a bit, I plan to use My Loyal Knights on you, Tarte. If I do, you'll have to stay with me for the rest of your life. Are you okay with that?" I asked.

"M-my entire life? Th-that sounds amazing! Please use it on me. I belong to you, Lord Lugh!"

Tarte excitedly balled her fists in front of her chest. She looked adorable.

"Let's head back. Tomorrow's going to get very busy. You'll need to pay more attention to your conduct than usual because of who we'll be interacting with," I cautioned.

"You can count on me. I've practiced thoroughly to keep from embarrassing you."

Judging by how Tarte had carried herself at the academy, I had nothing to fret over. She had always been reliable. Truthfully, I was more likely to commit a breach of etiquette than she was.

While I'd gained some new abilities today, there were a few more souvenirs I intended on making mine before returning home. If the government was going to shove me into a deadly role, then I was going to get what I could from it.

Chapter 7 | The Assassin Rejects a Proposal

Eager to test out what I had received from Epona's My Loyal Knights, I immediately borrowed the castle training grounds. After performing some drills, I found that my physical ability was leagues above where it had been.

The most striking improvement was my mana discharge. I had a little over one thousand times the capacity of the average mage, but my immediate release being only ten times higher than the median was a weakness. Now, however, I could output twice as much as I had just yesterday, dramatically increasing what I could do in battle.

"I can't keep up with you at all, my lord…," Tarte remarked, falling to her knees as she panted.

She was acting as my sparring partner. I fought her at her full strength while intentionally not empowering myself with mana. Previously, that would have ensured my loss, but not anymore.

"I can't believe how strong I've become. I'm looking forward to using My Loyal Knights on you, Tarte."

"Me too. I love the idea of something of yours flowing inside of me and connecting us forever."

Is it just my imagination, or did that sound a little lewd?

Although I wanted to use My Loyal Knights on Tarte right away, I needed to conduct more tests. The goal was to gain some control over the skills I gave her. There were a few clear picks

I wanted to ensure she received—namely, Limitless Growth and Rapid Recovery. The combination was downright unfair.

The battle with General Orc had forced me to accept that demons were not the sort of things you could fight while remaining in the confines of human capability. That's why I wanted Tarte to gain powers that surpassed what most had.

In addition to two of my skills, I hoped to provide Tarte with Possibility Egg. Once I'd figured out whether I could control My Loyal Knights, I'd use it on her.

"I feel very guilty about taking one of your three slots...but I still really want you to pick me," Tarte admitted bashfully.

"There's no reason not to. You're family, Tarte, and an important assistant."

Initially, I had taken her in only as a tool. That wasn't how I saw her anymore, though. Perhaps it was shameless to think as much after conditioning the girl to ensure her undying loyalty, but I believed our bond was genuine.

"Thank you! You are everything to me, my lord. Do you know who the other two will be?"

"One will be Dia."

As my lover, Dia would be with me forever. Even excluding that, she was the most skilled mage I knew. I had no reason not to pick her.

"And the other?"

"That's a little difficult. The safe choice would be Maha. But she doesn't need combat strength. It could also be Dad if I wanted instant firepower... I'll put that decision on hold until it becomes necessary."

I only had three uses of My Loyal Knights. There was no need to decide them all right away. I actually preferred having one slot open.

"Personally, I think Maha would be a good choice. She likes you as much as I do," Tarte stated.

"That does merit consideration. Let's head back. Dinner will be soon."

"I suddenly feel very nervous. I'll do my best not to embarrass you, my lord."

Tarte's skills as a maid were excellent, so I was sure she'd be fine.

The dinner was not arranged by the royal family but by another noble household staying within the royal castle. All aristocrats visiting the palace and their respective kin were in attendance, and each of the fifty guests had the power to eradicate House Tuatha Dé at the mere lift of a finger.

As the man of the hour, I drew all eyes when I entered. Their gazes then moved to Mom, Tarte, and Dia. Those present were no strangers to beautiful women, but even then, these three stood out.

It was a source of pride but also unease. Tarte looked wholly flustered, but Mom and Dia were used to the attention.

Out of those assembled, I recognized Naoise Gephis. He was a classmate of mine and the heir to one of the four major dukedoms of the Alvanian Kingdom. When I glanced his way, he winked.

"I humbly thank you for inviting us to this banquet tonight," my dad said. Then he bowed, and we followed his example.

We were ordered to sit, and Tarte stationed herself behind me. Considering our rank, we should have been at the foot of the table. However, we were granted seats of honor.

"Baron Tuatha Dé, I apologize for pulling you away from your preparations for the award ceremony. I wanted to ask your son some questions," Duke Gephis explained with a shallow, pleasant smile.

The man possessed a medium build, and his hair was streaked with gray. His chiseled face gave the impression of intelligence. Although his attire was fancy, there was no hint of pretentiousness about him.

A quick look around revealed that most of the nobles here appeared to be upstanding people. That was likely because Duke Gephis, the sponsor of the dinner, had selected them.

I suppose birds of a feather do flock together. Do honorable aristocrats attract one another, or are they all subordinates that Duke Gephis educated himself?

We didn't have to wait long to be served our meal.

"Now I get it," I muttered.

Three appetizers were brought to the table: a dish consisting of walnuts sprinkled onto an edible plant called a sobier, berry sauce–coated meat from a large bird called a Harta pheasant, and raw Grasake salmon, all things which could only be found in the north.

The entrée was cuisine from the same region—bear meat stewed in a local style of miso. Even the bread was made of rye, known for growing well in colder temperatures. Every ingredient had been imported from the Gephis domain, as had the cook. This was despite the fact that you could have anything made for you at the royal castle at a simple request.

The act was meant as a statement against the central government. Gephis and his followers refused to accept the decision to keep the hero here.

"How do you like this food? Does it suit your tastes better than the cuisine of the capital?" Gephis asked me.

"It's delicious, but the capital's local fare isn't bad, either."

The duke was really asking whether I would align myself with the north, or more specifically, House Gephis. My reply told him that I couldn't accept the proposal at the moment.

The atmosphere of the room became a little tense, and my dad spoke up.

"Let's quit this roundabout way of speaking typical of the central government. There is no one eavesdropping on us, and I can guarantee that none of my family will betray this conversation to others. Unless there happens to be an informant mixed in among your honorable guests, Duke Gephis, we should be fine."

Some did not take my dad's words so well, standing up in outrage.

"There's no chance any of us would betray the duke!"

"You're pushing your luck, Baron Tuatha Dé!"

Duke Gephis scowled at the nobles who lost their composure, and they quietly sat back down. He had them well disciplined.

"I apologize for my subordinates. They tend to be the worrying sort."

The indirect message was to prevent anything said here from being used as evidence against us. If Duke Gephis asked for my allegiance directly, it could be seen as treason.

None of that mattered, though, so long as our exchange was never leaked.

"Then I'll ask directly. We don't consent to the central government's decisions. Are you actually capable of killing demons?" Duke Gephis peered into my eyes.

"I don't know. I was able to slay the last one, but I couldn't keep it dead. No matter how many times I struck it down, it revived. Had Epona not been there, I would've had to run."

"Oh? You claim you were able to kill it, albeit not permanently. I find that hard to believe. How were you able to pull off such a thing?"

"I possess an S-Rank skill."

"And what kind of power does it give you?"

"I'm sorry, describing it would be the equivalent of announcing my weaknesses to the world. So I'm abstaining from answering that."

Only one out of every one hundred million people possessed

an S-Rank skill. Just having one made you one of the strongest people in the world.

"I understand. However, does your skill matter at all if you are unable to end demons permanently?"

"Since the battle, I have devised a method of slaying demons for good. The only problem is I have no way to verify that it works. I can't claim this method will be effective until the next time a demon appears. For now, all I can state is that there is a chance I can kill demons."

Hiding it now was pointless, so I was honest on that front.

"I see... If it does work, then that would be a truly monumental accomplishment. Not counting the hero, you would be the first person in history to slay a demon."

Duke Gephis understood how much this could mean. Others besides me might become able to kill demons, too.

"That's why I'd prefer you didn't have me die from some mysterious illness or accident and argue with the central government to release the hero. Instead, I ask that you bet on my success. You should know that I don't want to die and will resist any attempts on my life to the best of my ability. I have an S-Rank skill, so taking me out will prove difficult."

"Ha-ha-ha, looks like you saw right through me."

The duke planned to neutralize me so that the central government would have to revisit their decision to keep the hero for themselves. That's why there'd been people tailing our carriage during the trip to the royal capital.

"You are a fascinating boy. Baron Tuatha Dé, you were blessed with a remarkable child."

"Yes, Lugh is my pride and joy. However, that surely isn't the end of the discussion, is it?"

"That is correct. We have run out of patience with the central government in regard to this case. While the royal family still has good intentions, the central government has them completely under their thumb," Duke Gephis declared.

While Gephis's lands to the north and those regions to the south where Tuatha Dé was situated were made up of decent people, the same could not be said of the dukedoms to the east and west. Corrupt aristocrats populated them, and it was these people that Duke Gephis was referring to when he said "their thumb."

"If you really can kill demons, Lugh, your fame is only going to grow. To the extent that the east and west won't be able to ignore you. With you and the hero on our side, we could wipe out their influence. Will you lend us your strength? We will reward you and back you up with our full force."

Having the support of a prominent noble house would be extremely helpful in my efforts to eradicate demons. The backing of House Gephis would also give me the most power I could ever gain in noble society. Unfortunately, joining them would limit my freedom of choice, making this a difficult situation.

"You entreat me to stand by your side, but what exactly does that entail?" I pressed, hoping to stall for more time to think.

"We will tie House Gephis and House Tuatha Dé together in matrimony. There is no stronger bond than one of blood. My son Naoise will marry your lovely sister, Claudia," Duke Gephis explained.

"I decline your offer," I answered instantly.

Massive wealth and authority would fall House Tuatha Dé's way if we were to become connected to a duke's house. Conversely, if we refused this offer, we risked making a powerful enemy.

Even still, this idea was out of the question. Dia was mine. I'd decided that I would live my second life the way I wished. If accepting this deal meant losing the woman I loved, then it was no choice at all.

"Do you have the authority to give that answer? Should it not be the head of your house?" demanded Duke Gephis.

"No. Because what you need isn't the power of House Tuatha Dé, it's the strength of a second hero. I expect Dad will leave this to me," I replied.

"That's right. The decision is his."

Duke Gephis knit his eyebrows. He hadn't expected a rejection. From a practical standpoint, I had every reason to accept. He was treating us with the utmost kindness, going so far as to offer Naoise, his son and heir, to Dia rather than to any of the nobles in his service.

"...I see. That is disappointing, but I have high hopes for your endeavors. Let us meet after you slay a demon, and I may have a different offer for you," the duke said after a moment.

"I look forward to it."

"All right, that is the difficult talk out of the way. Now, please relax and enjoy your dinner. Our chef's dessert is exquisite."

"Thank you very much."

The man had dropped his offer right away. He saw from my response there was no hope of convincing me.

After that, everyone simply enjoyed the meal. Dia ended up really loving the northern cuisine. Seeing that, I discerned all the recipes used to make this type of cuisine for her in the future, and even better dishes.

I love Dia. I won't let anyone steal her from me, and I want to make her happy.

Chapter 8 | The Assassin Is Named a Holy Knight

Following the dinner with Duke Gephis, there were many more parties and social functions my family and I had to attend. As I'd expected, it all became exhausting before long.

A certain number among the nobility considered it a sign of status to leave the management of their domains to subordinates and then live in a villa in the royal capital. Going to gatherings with other aristocrats became the daily routine. I didn't know how they handled it.

"You're so popular, Lugh. In just a few days here, you've been flooded with wedding proposals."

"Mom, will you stop that? I'm tired enough already."

The only reason I was being sent around the country in Epona's place was to give the central government an excuse to keep her in the royal capital. I was a sacrificial pawn. Still, many took the central government's announcement at face value, and I was bombarded with offers of marriage wherever I went.

"Dia, you're getting lots of them yourself," I commented.

"I've passed on them all. It sickens me to even look at them," she replied.

Dia had turned down an impressive number of proposals while living in Viekone, so she probably hated these sorts of things even more than I did.

"Hmm-hmm-hmm, I'm actually glad to hear that," my mother said. "You should have seen your faces during the dinner."

Dia blushed slightly. "I was really touched, Lugh. You didn't hesitate at all."

I'd trained myself never to show emotion, but that had been a moment of weakness.

"...Please don't tease me too much."

"You're so cute today, Lugh," Dia remarked, and she reached over to hug me on the bed I was sitting on.

There was jealousy in Tarte's eyes. If she wanted to embrace me, too, she should have done so.

"We finally only have two more days. It feels like we've been here forever," I said.

Since arriving, it had been nothing but social functions. The medal ceremony was today, and once the afterparty concluded, we could finally head back to Tuatha Dé. We'd only been here for a short while, but I'd become quite homesick.

"This is your big moment, Lugh, so we need to dress you up nicely," my mom all but sang.

"Ah, I'll help with that. Ta-daa! I have a makeup kit. Even guys can look good when they put on a little," said Dia.

"Um, I'll do what I can, too," Tarte chimed in.

The three of them closed in on me. It was a bit frightening. Dad saw the scene unfolding and chuckled.

"...Dad, do you enjoy seeing me in pain?" I asked.

"No, I was just thinking about how you've always been so strangely mature from such a young age, but that all falls apart in front of them," he answered.

"Aren't you the same with Mom, Dad?"

"You're not wrong. It may always be the women who wear the pants in the Tuatha Dé household."

I couldn't accept that. As a man, I wanted to lead.

In the end, I was helpless against the mysterious power the girls of this family held, and they dressed me as they pleased. Fortunately, the end result wasn't so bad.

The ceremony to recognize distinguished service was being held within the castle before an audience with the king. As the stars of the show, Epona and I would go last.

Carriages had been coming and going endlessly from the castle since morning. Many guests were from foreign countries. As this ceremony concerned demon slaying, it was relevant to people of all nations.

Dia used makeup to disguise her face slightly as a precaution. There were visitors here from Viekone as well.

Someone called me from where I'd been waiting and guided me to the door leading to the throne room. Epona was already there. She was wearing a dignified men's blue and white outfit that befit the hero.

"Hello, Lugh. Have you been comfortable here in the capital?" she inquired.

"Honestly, I'm sick of going to party after party. I don't know how you put up with this lifestyle."

"Ah-ha-ha, you get used to it. How does my power feel?"

"I'm growing accustomed with time. The excessive strength threw me off at first, but with some work, I've become able to manage it."

All the might in the world didn't mean much if you couldn't control it. Managing my recent jump in physical ability was trying, but I was handling it well enough.

"That's good. You'll definitely be able to kill demons."

"Yeah. Even solo-type demons shouldn't be a problem for me now," I declared.

Demons fell into two categories, solo-type and commander-type. The latter were creatures like General Orc, who summoned countless underlings and crushed everything in their paths with overwhelming numbers. On the opposite side of things were solo-types, which couldn't create monsters but possessed unbelievable power.

Without Epona's gift, I still would have been able to defeat commander-type demons, but solo-types would have been difficult.

There's no doubt both kinds were a significant threat, regardless of their differences.

"Honored hero, Lord Lugh, please come this way," called a servant. He opened the door, meaning our time had come.

A red carpet extended to the throne, flanked on either side by attendees. I noticed a surprising face among the crowd—Maha. Perhaps a select number of prominent merchants had been invited to help make this a grand affair.

Maha had purposely kept her attendance a secret from me and stuck out her tongue when I locked eyes with her.

"I can't believe that girl."

Epona and I walked down the carpet together. It was embarrassing having everyone's eyes focused on us. When we reached the king, we knelt and bowed our heads.

The ruler of Alvan looked to be a timid and overly kind sort of person.

"Hero Epona. Raise your head," he commanded.

"Yes, Your Majesty," Epona replied, and she stood.

"You did splendidly in eradicating the demon during the recent battle. You rendered service befitting of your title. I hereby confer upon you these rewards."

The king then read out the list of Epona's compensation. A troubled look crossed her face when the king stated that everything would be delivered to her family's household. She was quick to erase that expression, however, and accepted the prizes graciously.

"Next, Lugh Tuatha Dé. You located the demon in the midst of all that chaos and guided the hero to it. You also routed more monsters than anyone, including the hero, and you continued to fight until the demon was slain. Despite not being the hero yourself, you demonstrated strength and prowess that rivals his own. This birth of this young legend is a blessing from the gods!"

The audience got even more excited for me than they had for Epona. Someone from a low-ranking noble family being treated as the hero's equal was the kind of success story that only existed in fairy tales. Anyone would have been delighted to be in my shoes. I was not all that pleased about this, however.

"Lugh Tuatha Dé, I bestow upon you the position of Holy Knight. You will receive privilege equal to that of the hero."

"I am much obliged."

Holy Knight. The name was a bit excessive. Being granted the same privileges as Epona was also a surprise. Her authority was far-reaching. With this, I'd be able to do just about anything I pleased.

"Come before me."

I obeyed the king and approached. He placed a necklace on

me. Strung on it was a pocket watch in the shape of a sword, a symbol of my new status.

"Lugh Tuatha Dé, I expect results in keeping with your new station. Go and wipe the demons from this land," proclaimed the king.

"I will give my best efforts to live up to your expectations, Your Majesty," I responded.

A few people started to clap, and the whole room quickly broke into thunderous applause. Had the situation been different, this may have been rather touching. Yet, considering I was tasked with killing creatures immortal against all but the hero, the standing ovation was like cheering at a funeral.

I had been searching for a way to kill demons, but the king and those in the audience didn't know that. Thinking about this was making my head hurt.

The rest of the ceremony played out as expected. We then moved to a dance hall, and the gathering turned into a grand party. Music sounded through the large chamber, and many people began to dance.

It wasn't long before I was surrounded and bombarded with questions. I stuck to safe answers to avoid making any comments that could be used against me. There were so many people approaching that I couldn't even find time to eat.

As soon as I finally felt like I'd have a chance to catch my breath, the music changed. A crowd of noble ladies rushed over to me, seeing it as an opportunity to invite me to waltz. All I wanted to do was slip away. Then I felt someone grab my hand.

"Would you allow me this dance?"

"Gladly, proxy representative of Natural You."

It was Maha. She couldn't have made an appearance at a more

opportune time. Waltzing with her would be much less stressful than with some girl I was barely acquainted with.

I'd learned how to dance a long time ago, specifically for infiltrating gatherings like this. Maha was also experienced in these matters, due to being the daughter of a wealthy merchant. She'd received a high-quality education before being orphaned and had plenty of chances to polish those skills while serving as my representative at Natural You.

"You seem tired, Sir Holy Knight."

She was using a different form of address with me than usual. Illig Balor and Lugh Tuatha Dé were separate people, and as far as anyone knew, this was the first time Lugh and Maha had met.

"What can I say? This kind of thing doesn't really suit me," I said in reply.

"I don't think that's true. Even surrounded by vanity and fantasy, you can dance skillfully."

"*Can* and *want to* are different things."

"Then what is it you're doing now?"

"I'm dancing because I want to. This isn't so bad when it's with you, Maha."

She looked stunning in her blue dress, and she radiated a mature sort of charm. This kind of womanly appeal was something Dia and Tarte couldn't match.

"Hee-hee, I'm glad to hear it. I have a prophecy for you. Good news will arrive soon."

"I like the sound of that."

Maha's ambiguous statement was likely referring to something I'd been seeking for a while using the Balor Company information network.

The music's intensity grew as it reached its climax, and the dancing quickened to match it.

A smile crossed Maha's face. Spending time with her like this released all the pent-up frustration building in me since arriving in the royal capital. It wasn't chance that we ended up dancing like this—Maha was worried about me and had sought me out faster than anyone else. I wanted to return the favor.

Using a special method of directed speaking so that others wouldn't overhear, I stated, "Maha, after returning home, I'll be heading to Milteu. I have some jobs to take care of."

"You're as busy as ever."

"I guess so. But after that, let's take a day to go on a date."

"That would be lovely. I'll dress up as nicely as I can. I'll make theater and restaurant reservations, too. And then…"

Her plans came out swift. It was shaping up to be an eventful day, but that wasn't a bad thing. Typically, I was always taking the lead. It was nice to be on the other side for a change.

I danced with Dia next, and before I knew it, the party was over. Despite the late hour, my family and I decided to head home now rather than wait until morning.

This trip had proven fruitful in several ways. The few chances I'd have to train during breaks in my cluttered schedule were going to be very important.

Chapter 9 | The Assassin Goes on a Date

Our long trip to the royal capital had ended, and we were on our way back to the Tuatha Dé domain. My dad and I took turns driving the carriage. At present, it was my turn, and Dia and Tarte were keeping me company. Dia seemed in a sour mood.

"I'm sorry. It's not that I forgot about our promise to go on a date. I just thought I would be able to make time for at least one day while we were there," I apologized.

"Hmph. I understand that in my head. That's why I'm not complaining. But my heart is a different matter. At least let me sulk."

I'd promised her time together in the royal capital as thanks for working so hard on developing the demon-killing spell. Unfortunately, we kept receiving invitations from nobles of higher standing and couldn't refuse. I'd hardly even had a free moment, much less time enough for a date.

Naoise took the one unoccupied moment I'd had. After the dinner with his father, he'd requested a secret meeting. Truly, his aspirations knew no bounds.

"I'll make up for it. I'm going to Milteu when we get back, so we'll go on a date for real this time."

Dia's face suddenly lit up as if she had never been upset. "Milteu! There were a lot of places we didn't visit last time."

Although I was only going to Milteu because of what Maha had said at the afterparty, taking Dia along seemed all right. I had something I wanted to prepare for her as well.

"But will that be okay, my lord? As a Holy Knight, you need to be able to head out immediately when you receive orders from the castle," Tarte said.

"It'll be fine. I'm only planning on staying there for one night. I won't be there for long."

A Holy Knight was required to head wherever demons appeared. I couldn't risk being out of contact for too long.

"Hmm-hmm, I'm looking forward to it. Where should we go?" asked Dia.

"If you have nowhere in mind, then I'll be your guide. I know that place like the back of my hand," I answered.

I'd lived in Milteu for two years as Illig Balor. It was practically my second hometown.

"All right, then it's a date. Having you show me around sounds great. Just so you know…I will be seriously depressed if it doesn't work out this time."

"I'll work hard to ensure that doesn't happen. If a demon appears near some town before we get to Milteu, we'll just have our date there."

"That would be fun in its own way, I guess. I don't get to go to the countryside very often."

"We don't ever have a need to."

Unless possessed of a love for travel, nobles didn't often enter domains other than their own.

Dia rubbed her eyes, looking sleepy.

"I'm sure you're tired. You should sleep. There's no need to push yourself," I said.

She'd wound up getting approached by a deluge of young male nobles at the party, likely as a result of her good looks. As a noble lady of the great House Viekone, she knew how to handle herself, but that kind of onslaught would tire out anyone. What's more, it was very late.

"Yeah, I think I'll do just that. Good night." No sooner had the words left Dia's mouth than she laid her head down in my lap and fell asleep.

I'd told Dia to get some rest, but I hadn't expected her to indulge herself in such a way. This did have its benefits, though. It gave me a front-row seat to Dia's adorable slumbering face.

Tarte glanced at Dia with envy.

Suddenly, Dia's eyes cracked open slightly. "You've always got that longing look in your eyes. If you want to do this, too, then just say so. That's a bad habit of yours, Tarte. If you plan on refraining, then keep your desire from showing on your face. Hoping Lugh will notice your feelings and then waiting for everything to fall into your lap is impudent and spoiled."

"I—I didn't intend anything like that...," Tarte mumbled, flustered.

"I want you to trust Lugh and me a little more. Just say what you want, and I won't get mad, okay?" Dia said.

"...Um, are you sure it's all right?"

"It's fine with me. I don't know what Lugh thinks, though."

"But..."

"Asking him is the only way to find out."

Dia was a bit tough with Tarte, but she was right. I found that straightforwardness to be one of her loveliest traits.

"U-um, Lord Lugh, can I rest my head on you, too?" Tarte timidly inquired.

"Sure, I don't mind. In exchange, can I use your lap when it comes time to switch coachmen?"

"Yes! I'm so excited."

Tarte then lay right down. Dia altered her position to make room for the other girl. Having two heads on my legs was quite heavy, but I felt strangely happy nonetheless.

All right, I feel energized. Let's hurry back home.

After arriving in the Tuatha Dé domain, everyone took a day to relax and refresh. Once I'd recuperated, it was time to make for Milteu.

"...Lugh. You've always been superhuman, but soon you're going to leave humanity behind altogether. How in the world were you able to get here from Tuatha Dé in just two hours?"

"I just ran with you in my arms, Dia."

Had I been traveling with a lot of luggage, I'd have taken a carriage. However, if I had no baggage, then running was swifter. I still had plenty of room in my Leather Crane Bag, so there was no need for cumbersome trunks. Plus, I'd wanted to test the new powers I'd gained from Epona.

"Lord Lugh, I'm so tired," Tarte groaned, and she sat down.

"That's fine. It's enough that you came with us," I replied.

By running ahead of Tarte, I served as her windbreak and lightened the trip's burden on her by a substantial amount. Still, not many could keep up with me.

"I was surprised I didn't fall behind, my lord. I'll go ahead and make reservations at our inn and deliver your message. Have fun on the date."

"Thanks, Tarte."

I'd asked her to meet with Maha ahead of me and take care of the necessary preparations. I doubted even Maha was expecting me to arrive in Milteu this quickly.

My date with Dia in Milteu was underway. We began by enjoying some cake at one of our favorite pastry shops.

"Mmm, the texture of this fresh cream is the best," Dia remarked.

"This place never disappoints," I responded.

This shop was on the expensive side, but not so much that it could be called a luxury establishment. The ingredients it used, however, were top-notch.

Most importantly, the chef was very skilled, especially with the fresh cream and sponge cake—their signature products. I preferred shops with true talent over those that simply constructed an extravagant atmosphere.

Dia and I sipped our tea as we enjoyed the cake.

"Oh, this is that tea you like," she said.

"Seems like this place has become a client of Natural You as well," I commented.

My cosmetics brand didn't just sell makeup; we also offered herbal tea and sweets, targeted mainly at wealthy women. I'd created this particular brew by purchasing a plantation overseas and then raising the leaves through selective breeding. They weren't obtainable from anyone other than Natural You.

Now that I think of it, Maha is a fan of this store, too.

The leaves should have been too expensive for the prices that this establishment sold the tea at. Maha probably sold to this place at a discount in exchange for greater publicity. This store was renowned and had a solid customer base.

The herbal brew tasted all the better when sampling it with this shop's fantastic cake. Undoubtedly, many would want to buy the tea for use at home. Maha was doing a great job.

"We need to buy a souvenir. I really do feel guilty... Next time, you should take Tarte on a date," Dia said.

"I've made preparations for us to pick up a gift when we leave for home, so don't worry about it. Still, I'm surprised to hear a girl tell me to go out with another girl," I responded.

"That's not something I would normally say. But Tarte is so sweet that I can't help but worry about her."

Above all, Dia thought of Tarte as a valuable friend. What she'd talked about in the carriage the other day was for Tarte's sake.

"...Also, I feel like I have some room to get away with saying things like that. The reason I'm comfortable with Tarte getting close to you is that I know I'm your number one. If that weren't the case, I would probably get jealous."

"Huh. I'm glad you told me how you feel. All right, let's get moving. On to the next location. This date is just getting started."

"Yeah, let's go."

We held hands and left the shop.

Dia gazed up at me with excitement in her eyes.

"That was amazing. It's hard to believe they did all that without casting any spells. Cutting a person in half without killing them, teleporting across the stage—it was all fantastic. Halfway through, I tried to detect mana because I couldn't believe they weren't using magic!"

We'd gone to see an illusion show. Nobles went to the theater all the time, so I assumed Dia would be tired of that. Thus, I thought this would be a good change of pace. This sort of act had come from overseas recently and was becoming very popular. From Dia's expression, it appeared she'd enjoyed it even more than I'd expected.

"It was fun," I said.

"Did you understand how they did any of it, Lugh?" Dia questioned.

"Yeah, I know how every trick was done."

"No way. Tell me, then."

"For the one where they sawed a person in half, they used a special bed with a blanket covering the legs, which prevented us from seeing under it. That's how they pulled off the illusion. There were actually two people in the bed, both bending their bodies at the waist. The person playing the top half of the body had the bottom half of their body hidden below the bed, and the person playing the bottom half of the body did the opposite. The blade went in between them, so it didn't truly cut anything."

"Ah, that makes sense."

While the trick was very simple, it was tough to notice.

"All right, what about the teleportation?"

"They used twins. There was a hidden door on the stage with enough room for one person to hide behind. Remember how they threw a card high up into the air and then waved a cloth around? They were drawing the audience's attention toward the fabric. The first twin used that moment to jump into the hidden door, and the other twin emerged from another concealed exit on a different part of the stage. It's common to conduct this trick with a secret passage, but these performers took advantage of having twins by making the second one appear instantly to increase dramatic impact."

"How did you know it was twins?" Dia pressed, hungry for more.

"If you looked closely, you could see they had slight differences in appearance that suggested they were separate people, and their clothing only made it more obvious. To the untrained eye, they were wearing the same outfit, but there were differences in the sheen of the leather, the cleanliness, the seams, and more."

"...Even in matters unrelated to magic, mana, and physical prowess, you really are inhuman, Lugh."

Dia's words almost wounded me.

"Do you feel better knowing the secrets behind their tricks?" I asked.

"Yeah, I do. But it's impressive you saw through all of that."

"It's a habit of mine. The techniques behind illusions can be divided into two extremes. The first is to deceive the audience by creating a blind spot, and the second is to direct the crowd's attention to something else in order to keep them from seeing what's really happening. It's the same in my profession. When someone tries to guide my eyes a certain way, I instinctively look in the other. If I didn't do that while on a job, it would mean death. That's how I discovered the secrets to their act."

The similarities between assassination and illusions went beyond basic ideology. There was a decent number of killing techniques that looked like prestidigitation. Because of that connection, I'd learned a fair number of magic tricks in my past life.

It served as good training for my creative thinking, awareness, and dexterity.

"You really can do anything... Do you by chance know how to do illusions even better than the ones we saw today?"

"I do."

"Then please show me sometime! Let's throw a party at the estate. Not the aristocrat kind, though, just the sort where you hang out with your family. You can put on an amazing show for us."

"That sounds fun. Would you be willing to help me with that? I'd need an assistant."

"Hmm, as long as there's nothing that looks painful like getting cut in half, then sure."

"You'll be a big help. Illusions look better the more beautiful the assistant."

"Oh, don't make me blush."

Dia squeezed an arm tightly around mine. We then set off walking through the streets together at night. We'd finished with everything I'd planned for today, and all we had left to do was return to the inn.

Somewhere along the way, Dia came to a sudden halt.

I turned to look at her. "Something wrong?"

"Hey, Lugh, can we make a stop on the way back?"

Dia had stopped in front of a love hotel. These kinds of establishments were rare in rural areas like Tuatha Dé, but cities had them in abundance.

"Um, with Tarte and Esr...Mom around at the estate, I've been too shy to ask you for this kind of thing, but here...," she whispered with a face flushed pitifully red.

It might have been my imagination, but she smelled sweeter than usual.

"I don't mind, but if we go in, I don't think I'll be able to restrain myself. Are you okay with that?" I questioned.

"...Stop asking me that kind of thing. I'm already so embarrassed, I feel like I'm going to die."

True to her words, Dia had already become unable to look at me and was casting her eyes down to the ground.

I'd wanted to sleep with Dia for a while, but I had been too afraid of what I might do once I lost myself to lust and had refrained thus far. Yet, if I didn't take her now after what she'd said, I'd be unworthy of being called a man.

"I'll be as gentle as I can, Dia." I took her hand without waiting for a reply. Dia didn't lift her eyes from the ground, but she returned my grip with a tight one of her own.

I guess it's finally time, I thought, gulping.

I'd had sex plenty of times, both in this life and my last one. Yet this would be my first time with someone I loved. Admittedly, I was nervous, more than I had been in my entire life. Even when I'd killed presidents, I hadn't been so anxious.

Thankfully, I knew an assassination technique to prevent any of that from showing on my face. I was sure that if I looked apprehensive, it would only serve to frighten Dia.

Chapter 10 | The Assassin Performs a Promotion

My first date with Dia in a while had turned out to be a lot of fun... Then she and I finally took the next step forward together.

I wanted to be gentle and not push her too hard because it was her first time. However, such thoughts quickly disappeared from my mind.

Dia was too cute, and I lost the ability to hold back. The end result left Dia exhausted, so I suggested we stay overnight in the love hotel. She rejected that, however. It seemed she didn't like the idea of Tarte growing suspicious. That was a little unexpected, as I didn't think Dia was the type to worry about that kind of thing.

The three of us were having breakfast at the inn Tarte had set us up in. It was plain to everyone that Dia's behavior was a little off. She was constantly spacing out and blushing.

"Lady Dia, are you not feeling well? It's been a little while since you've eaten anything," Tarte inquired.

"No, it's nothing like that. I feel fine. Just fine. Yeah."

"If you're not feeling well, then please let me know. Ah, you have a bug bite. There's a red spot on your neck. Maybe that's the reason. I also noticed you were walking a little strangely."

"N-no, that's not— I'm telling you, I'm fine!"

Her strange conduct likely had to do with what happened last night. I was having trouble concentrating, too. I had no idea that sleeping with someone I loved felt so fulfilling.

My eyes met Dia's, and we stared at each other for a few seconds. Tarte looked at us and tilted her head in confusion.

Hastily, I cleared my throat. "Tarte, tell me how yesterday went."

"Yes, my lord! I went to speak to Maha. After that, I cleaned our house. It was so dirty that it made me think I should take regular trips there."

The house she was referring to was the estate I'd lived in during my time as Illig Balor. Maha still resided there. Her work was very demanding, so it wasn't astonishing to learn she had no time for tidying up. Maha made more than enough money to hire someone to do it for her, of course, but there were things in that house we couldn't let others see.

"I see. That was probably for the best. I'm going to head out. You two do whatever you want."

I was going to meet Maha as Illig Balor. Thus, I couldn't be seen with Tarte or Dia.

"Understood. Lady Dia, should I show you around like last time?" Tarte suggested.

"…I'll pass. Walking is a little rough right now. I'm going to relax here and read a book or something. Enjoy yourself, and don't worry about me, Tarte."

"I knew it. You really aren't feeling well."

"Once again, I'm fine. There's nothing to fret over."

This was my fault. I'd offered to use mana to increase Dia's self-healing, but she insisted that she wished to feel the pain.

"Then I will leave you here, Lady Dia. I'm going to go shopping. Lady Esri requested some things from me. Once I finish that, I'll get a bunch of sweets that you like and return. Please tell me if there's anything else you want," Tarte said.

"Thanks, that would be great."

Both the girls seemed like they could manage without me.

Maha was eagerly awaiting my arrival, and I wanted to get my hands on the item I'd requested her to obtain for me. It could make a massive difference in my fight against demons.

When I arrived at Maha's office, I was immediately greeted by a giant stack of papers being shoved in my face.

"Can you take care of those documents for me, dear brother? I wish you had given me at least a week's notice before coming to see me. That way, I would have been able to make more time. If I don't finish all of this by the end of the day, Natural You's business will stagnate."

A second mountain of sheets was piled high on Maha's desk.

"Sorry about that. I just couldn't sit still after you told me you'd found what I've been after. And more importantly, I wanted to sit and talk with you. We haven't gotten the chance in a while," I replied.

"…You can be so simpleminded. I didn't think you would get that excited over just a couple of words."

Wasting no time, we both got to work.

Maha was busy. She had a lot on her plate as my representative at Natural You, and she provided support for my assassination jobs to boot. Securing time alone with her was tough, but that's why I'd come today. Natural You was my company, so obviously, I could help out with Maha's work.

As my representative, Maha was responsible for steering the

enterprise along the best possible course. Together, we went through approving, rejecting, and deferring various documents. Looking through the papers made me realize Natural You had grown far beyond what I had envisioned. Maha was truly adept.

After some time of silently working through the avalanche of sheets, a visitor stopped by.

"Long time no see, Illig."

"Hey, it certainly has been a while. How long has it been since we've talked, Beruid?" I answered, taking care not to speak like Lugh anymore.

Beruid Balor, Illig's older brother, wore a gentle smile on his face. He was set to inherit the Balor Company, and for reasons I didn't fully understand, he also worked for Natural You. Still grinning, he dropped more papers on the heap.

"I have something I wish to talk about, but first, please finish up your business here," the man said.

"...Beruid, I came here on a different matter. It would help if you could push all nonessential items to a later date, if at all possible."

"These are essential matters. Maha pushed aside quite a lot to make it to the party at the royal castle, and now we're in a tight spot."

"I would have preferred you didn't mention that," Maha remarked with an embarrassed expression.

Attending the party at the royal castle had meant she'd lost a few days. During that time, things had piled up, literally.

Making appearances at important events was part of Maha's responsibilities. Celebrations like the award ceremony provided chances to hobnob and make connections with nobles and industrial big shots. However, Maha had mainly visited the royal capital because of me.

She really does have a lot on her plate. I need to do something sooner rather than later. I suppose I can just go ahead with that idea I've been mulling over. That should move this along.

I paused my work and turned toward Beruid. "Using my authority, I name Beruid vice-representative of the brand. Your authority is now equal to Maha's, but she retains precedence in all matters."

Swiftly, I drew up a contract, filling out the necessary components and adding my seal. Then I shoved the sheet at Beruid. He was at a loss for words, but I ignored that.

"I've decided to upgrade you from Maha's aide to a fellow helmsperson. That means you now have the right to approve or reject these documents. Would you mind assisting us?"

"U-uh, is that truly okay?"

"Natural You is my company. That means what I say goes. I've been planning on promoting you for a while. Maha has spoken highly of your work, as have subordinates and clients. Their compliments are what convinced me you are worthy of this position."

Maha was tackling too much alone. Most people would've cracked merely under the pressure of running Natural You, yet she also gathered intel and procured rare goods for me.

I wanted to lighten that load somehow. The quickest way was to leave the day-to-day operation of Natural You to another. Fortunately, Beruid was extremely skilled, and I trusted him on a personal level, too. The man was a mediocre self-starter, but he showed a talent for maintaining and growing already existing businesses.

"...I am so grateful for your offer. Honestly, I've been feeling very frustrated lately. Maha has taught me so much about your way of thinking, Illig. My job has been fulfilling and full of surprises, but at the same time, I always had the sense my talents were being wasted on the sidelines."

"I assumed that was the case. I want you to make full use of your ability from now on."

It was great to see Beruid so eager to prove himself. He was going to make Maha's life a lot easier.

The three of us then started going through the documents at a quick pace. Fortunately, it looked like we'd finish with enough time for me to be with Maha for a bit.

"The end is finally in sight," I commented.

"This really is much faster with three people," Maha added.

"It's mostly due to how absurdly fast you two are," Beruid said, looking at us with an expression of astonishment.

I trusted that he'd catch up after a while. It was simply a matter of getting used to it.

When at last everything was completed, I stood and proposed we all take a short tea break.

Beruid turned to Maha and me with strong resolve plain in his eyes. "Uh, Illig, Maha. I have a matter I want to discuss with you." Despite his determination, the man's voice trembled slightly. Beruid usually had nerves of steel; it was rare to see him act this way.

"All right, that's no problem. We'll make tea and then discuss," I declared.

"I second that idea. I'm very thirsty," said Maha.

We'd listen to what Beruid had to say. Then, once he was done, Maha and I would be alone, and I could finally get what I'd come here for.

At last, a new trump card. Or, more accurately, the materials for one.

It was something I'd used all the time in critical moments during my previous life. With it, I'd be able to make better use of my skills. Honestly, it was incredibly fortunate that Maha had done this for me before a demon appeared.

Chapter 11 | The Assassin Obtains a Long-Awaited Item

I brewed some tea using leaves Maha had obtained from a new trade route that she opened. They were from a different country than the tea Natural You sold. Apparently, where it came from, people drank it nonfermented like green tea. However, I thought it would be better fermented like black tea after tasting it. That not only improved the flavor but also gave it better nutritional value.

"This brew is really acidic. It's good for when you're tired, but I don't think this taste is for everyone. The smell is even harsher. It's pungent and a little sharp," Maha observed.

"I agree. I need to work on it a little before we introduce it to our stores. Hmm... Rather than making it palatable to a wide market, maybe I should increase the acidity and boost its medicinal effects. It already helps alleviate fatigue. Perhaps we could sell it as a stimulant people could take to squeeze a few more hours of work out of themselves."

All I had to do was tinker with how the tea leaves were processed to achieve that.

"Do you think our customers would be interested in that?" Beruid asked.

"Even if they aren't, soldiers will probably want it. If demons and monsters appear more going forward, sales for luxury items will decrease. That trend has already begun. Even the nobility's expenditure on finery is lessening as they begin to make military preparations. We can make up for that loss by entering a different market," I responded.

That was only an idea, but I was confident it would work.

"I like it. With armies all over suddenly on standby, we'll be able to sell to them regularly and in large quantities. Monopolizing the market would be great for business, too. This has a good chance of success, considering the medicinal effects. I'll take care of sales," Maha stated.

"You've done it again, Illig. You were able to sniff out a chance for profit from a single cup of tea. I need to learn from your example," said Beruid.

I was adept at this sort of thing. Herbs could be made into medicine or poison, depending on the species. My life as an assassin made me proficient with plants.

"I'll work on the tea leaves at my other home and send them to Maha once I'm finished. Also, Maha. If possible, can you purchase the land and tenant farmers where the tea leaves are made like you did last time?" I requested.

"Got it. I didn't expect you to like them this much."

"It's because of the medicinal effects. This is a variety that's very difficult to obtain on this continent."

Knowledge and talent wouldn't get you anywhere without the right materials. If these tea leaves were unobtainable in this region, I wanted to stock as much as possible.

Business aside, I also desired them for personal reasons.

"Sure thing. It seems like Beruid will be taking over most of my regular duties, so my schedule is free," replied Maha.

"I'll do my best. I also want to try my hand at starting

something new, but unfortunately, my plans still need a lot of work. Until then, I'll put all my focus into maintaining and growing the business," Beruid declared.

"I know you two will do great. Oh yeah, you said you had something you wanted to ask about, Beruid. Now that we've quenched our thirst, do you mind telling us what it is?"

Judging from Beruid's exaggerated behavior earlier, it seemed like a relatively serious matter.

"Thank you very much. I'd planned on only bringing this to Maha, but I thought that wouldn't be fair, so I decided I would do it in your presence, too."

Beruid's expression suddenly grew serious. He looked at Maha, then at me.

"Maha, will you marry me? I would like to receive your blessing, Illig."

Maha and I exchanged glances. This was a total shock for me, but she seemed composed. She turned a sad look at Beruid.

"This is unexpected. I would never have thought the distinguished son of the Balor family would say such words to a commoner like me. Don't you have a more worthy match? For you and for the Balor Company."

"There is no girl I want more than you, Maha. As we've worked together, I've come to love you from the bottom of my heart. I don't care about your standing. Your skill has more value to me than your place in society or your wealth. I admire your beauty and strength. My intentions are serious."

"So you are. Then I'll give you a serious answer. I'm sorry, but no."

Maha bowed in apology. She'd answered instantly, without any hesitation.

Rejecting a proposal from the son of the Balor Company should have been unthinkable, and yet, she had. Accepting would have made her one of the wealthiest people in the world. She could have reclaimed her father's company.

"I would ask for the reason...but I don't need to, do I? I understand. But I'll say this. You're a coward, Illig. You're aware of her feelings, and yet you ignore them. You hold her hostage by doing so... I'm leaving."

"Wait, Beruid," I called.

"Don't worry. I'll do my job. I can separate love and work. I have my pride as a merchant." Making those his final words, he left.

I can't believe he proposed to Maha. Actually, it's really not so strange. She is a very attractive girl.

"Maha, are you okay with that? If you wedded the successor of the Balor Company, you'd be able to do any kind of business you want. You'd finally achieve your dream."

"It's fine. I am yours, dear Illig," she replied before hugging me.

Despite what had just happened, she seemed as she always did, perhaps even more cheerful than usual.

"I knew it. Being proposed to did make you happy, didn't it?" I questioned.

"What do you mean, you 'knew it'? You're wrong. I'm pleased because you got jealous, dear brother. You're supposed to be acting as Illig right now, but you look so thoroughly shaken. Have you not noticed that your tone of voice has returned to normal?" countered Maha.

"That's embarrassing. I still have a ways to go."

I couldn't deny that Beruid popping the question had left me feeling a little off. The idea of Maha being stolen from me felt like getting clubbed in the head.

Nothing had ever flustered me this much in my previous life, even the threat of death. Perhaps this was the result of living as a human instead of a tool.

"I'm always envious of Dia and Tarte, so this is a nice feeling. It's only right that you know what it feels like now and then. Just yesterday, I had to hear about how you went to that hotel with your cute girlfriend."

"How do you know about that?"

"This city is the center of my information network. I learn of everything that happens here, even if you're acting as Lugh."

"…You really are the best."

"That's right. I'm useful, so don't forget about me. If you don't tie me down, I may just get up and leave someday," Maha warned.

"What can I do to prevent that?" I asked.

"There is only one method of tying a woman down."

I understood what Maha was asking for, but I couldn't give that to her. Instead, I tried to change the topic. "I brought you a present. It's those krulone cream puffs you liked."

"Ha-ha, I think you're still underestimating me. I'll let it go for now. I'm a very patient girl."

"Sorry."

"But don't think I'll wait forever."

"I'll keep that in mind."

I'd seen to an uncomfortable extent how much a person's emotions could change. That was why I knew not to take Maha's love for granted.

"That's lovely to hear. Let's move on to the main subject. I finally obtained the dried marche mushrooms you've been asking for. Tribes to the far south use them to enter a trancelike state during their ceremonies held to commune with the dead."

Maha pulled some of the fungi out of a bag and laid them out. I crushed them with a finger and rolled them over my tongue.

"...This is it. I can use these to make my secret weapon," I said.

"What exactly are you going to do with these?" Maha questioned.

"I'm going to make a drug. Do you remember the medicine I crafted that removes the limits on my brain and temporarily increases my mana discharge?"

That compound was the reason I'd survived the demon attack at the academy.

"Yeah. I worked really hard obtaining all of the ingredients for it."

"These mushrooms can be made into something similar. The effects will increase my concentration to its utmost limit and raise the processing power of my brain."

"What use would you have for something like that?"

"I've become a little too strong. I can't keep up with my own body. This drug should allow me to unleash all of my strength when I'm faced with a powerful enemy. There's also a certain skill I want to experiment with. I need to plumb its very depths. Watching the hero fight taught me something, and the key to matching her will be high mental ability. I can't do that without this substance."

My goal was to craft something based on the refined narcotics of my previous world. Scouring through old legends and records of ceremonies, I'd sought out the ingredients I required.

Tasting the mushrooms left no doubt in my mind. They were

exactly what I'd been looking for. If I mixed them with a few other chemicals I'd already had waiting, I'd have the compound I sought. As it happened, the tea leaves I'd treated Maha and Beruid to today were also part of the mixture.

"Seems dangerous. But considering what you're trying to do, dear brother, it is necessary. I'll hurry to get the foundation for a stable supply established," Maha stated dutifully.

"Sounds good. Sorry for relying on you so much."

I ask for way too much from Maha. Someday, I'll need to return the favor.

"That's all right. I receive plenty of compensation. Let's go on a date. You went on one with your cute girlfriend yesterday, and you can't refuse me after I've done so much for you, right? We have a reservation at a delicious restaurant."

"Okay, I'll get Dia and Tarte, too."

"No. I said a date. I also have a room at a hotel waiting, but I'll cancel that. Knowing your personality, I'm sure sleeping with another girl the day after your first experience would be impossible for you, dear brother."

"Thank you for your consideration."

Maha's eyes narrowed, and she put a finger to her lips. "You're welcome. Hmmm, judging from that response, I feel like it could happen if I just give you time to find room in your heart to justify it. That will be the moment I ensnare you."

I had to be cautious. Having that sort of relationship with Maha wasn't disagreeable, but I didn't like engaging in unplanned activities.

"It's easy to be on my best behavior around Dia and Tarte, but you've always got me at your whim, Maha," I remarked.

"If you're looking for a submissive woman who supports her

man...I don't think I can beat either of them on that front. So I've got to fight my own way. In keeping with that, allow me to take the lead on our date."

Maha and I had a great time together. Letting your partner take the initiative occasionally wasn't so bad.

I was glad I got the materials I needed for the drug before I fought any demons. Undoubtedly, it would make a huge difference. I also thought there was a chance I'd be able to choose the skills I gave to Dia and Tarte using My Loyal Knights while on the drug.

As soon as I was back in Tuatha Dé, I intended to get to work mixing and testing the narcotic.

Chapter 12 | The Assassin Is Targeted

Now done with our business in Milteu, I decided we should return home in a carriage. Running home would be much faster, but I had a reason for my decision.

"Dia, Tarte, what do you think the most frightening thing in noble society is?"

"Hmm, maybe political power. Or money!"

"I agree with Lady Dia. Nobles don't even think of people like us as humans. Ah, but House Tuatha Dé is completely different."

Influence and wealth were definitely symbols of an aristocrat's might.

"Incorrect. There is reason to be afraid of money and political power, but the mere possession of them isn't something to be feared. The problem is how they're used. Three principles govern a noble's conduct: the desire to move up in society, vanity, and jealousy. The third one is especially troublesome. You can control the other two to an extent, but there's nothing you can do about envy."

"...Ah, I see what you're saying." Dia nodded in understanding. She'd been raised as a major noble, so she grasped my words quickly. Tarte, however, tilted her head to one side, confused.

"When consumed by jealousy, aristocrats tend to become

aggressive. Initially, they might only badmouth the object of their ire, and then they'll start spreading false rumors. If that doesn't sate them, they may move on to traps or something more direct," I explained.

"Um, what do you mean by direct?" Dia asked.

"They'll try to eliminate the pest that has become such an eyesore. Should the target be of a lower standing, they can squash them easily. I don't think aristocrats can stand the idea of someone beneath them possessing something they don't."

Regardless of the world, the tallest blade of grass was the first to be cut.

Egotism inspired bigotry in the nobility, and their reckless use of power led to some serious character flaws. Still, being jealous of me because I was chosen as a Holy Knight seemed a little absurd. The central government was only using me as an excuse to keep the hero in the royal capital.

"Hmm, so that's why you chose to return home in a carriage and why you brought that up," Dia stated, having figured it out.

"Nice job. Some dangerous-looking people have been tailing us since this morning. They've evaded revealing themselves thus far, so they're quite skilled."

"I wonder if they're just observing us," offered Dia.

"I don't think that's it. Were that the case, I wouldn't feel such bloodlust coming off them."

Many people were interested in the new Holy Knight. Most of the time, they were content to watch. However, I was an assassin, and I could sense murderous intent in my bones. Those following our carriage wanted to kill.

"Um, then why did we leave the city in this buggy in the

middle of the night? It's like you're telling them to attack us, my lord," Tarte pointed out.

"That's precisely what I'm doing. This is bait. Being stalked until who knows when would be uncomfortable, right? So I'm having them make a move. I'll turn the tables and capture them, then force them to confess who they work for."

I needed to identify whoever wanted me dead and eliminate them swiftly.

"But will this really work out?" Dia asked doubtfully.

"That depends. Fortunately, it looks like they've laid a trap for us. See the two trees on either side of the highway about three hundred meters ahead? Look carefully between them."

The two girls did as instructed and gathered mana in their Tuatha Dé eyes.

"Ah, there's a string there."

"I'd feel awful for the horse if we crashed into that."

A tough metallic thread was tied taut between the trees. The sun had already set, so no one but me could have noticed. If the horse struck the wire, it would go tumbling over, and our carriage would crash to the ground.

"My plan is to charge into their ambush."

Dia's eyes widened in recognition. "I get what you're thinking now, Lugh. Going through the trap is the only way to get them to attack."

"That's correct. Let's take a tumble. Don't worry. I'll guide the horse so that it falls gently," I said.

"That's not what I'm worried about!!" Dia snapped.

We'd borrowed this steed. Any injury meant paying large indemnities. Considering Natural You's wealth, it was a small price to pay, but I still didn't enjoy wasting money. I intended to steer the horse with meticulous caution to ensure a graceful fall.

"I suppose you two should know what we're up against. The assailants trying to kill me are fairly adept."

Whoever wanted me dead likely believed my accomplishments during the battle with General Orc were fabricated. Even so, they had to know I was the best in my class and that I'd defeated a vice-commander of the Royal Order one-on-one. They weren't going to throw amateurs at me.

"Yeah, I think you're right," agreed Dia.

"I thought this would make for excellent practice, so I'm leaving them to you two," I declared.

The girls' eyes opened wide at that.

"What? We're going to fight them?" Dia asked.

"I-I'm not sure we can do it," Tarte admitted.

"You'll be fine. There are three people pursuing us, and each is as strong as a vice-commander of the Royal Order. Knowing that, it's safe to assume the person behind this is a major noble."

A mage's strength was primarily determined by the amount of mana they were born with. Thus, aristocrats engaged in selective breeding to maintain strong bloodlines.

This resulted in capable children who brought wealth to their houses, and much was invested in their education. Strength and political power tended to be proportionate to each other in Alvan.

Being attacked by foes of this caliber worked out very nicely for me. After all, if they had noble blood, then surely they knew something of use.

"This doesn't sound fine to me!" Again, Dia protested.

"I'm telling you, it won't be a problem. They're no better than vice-commanders. With how strong you two have become, your victory is assured. All right, it's time to fall. Be careful not to bite your tongue."

A few seconds later, the horse walked into the thread.

I slowed the horse as much as I could without tipping off our pursuers and skillfully directed it to tumble safely without injuring its legs. Next, I detached the steed and had the carriage collapse exactly as our opponents hoped.

There was a loud neigh as the startled horse stood and ran off.

All right, that went great. From their point of view, it looks like their trap got us.

That's when a giant fireball came our way. The spell threatened to send the buggy up in flames in an instant.

Only those who'd been educated from a young age could use that sort of magic. These assailants had to be the children of the head of their house.

"Ugh, fine. You'd better save us if this goes poorly, okay?"

Dia raised a scream, and towering walls of dirt rose from the ground to surround the carriage. It was an original earth spell of ours. We'd simplified the chant as much as possible so that the barricade could be erected in only two seconds.

The fireball was scorching, but its lack of mass caused it to bounce off the earth wall without breaking through it. In the briefest moment, Dia had selected the correct spell and executed it artfully. Her situational decision-making was excellent.

"I'll be watching from a distance. Just relax, and you'll win this fight." As soon as I said that, I used magic to burrow into the ground and slip from the scene in an undetectable way.

Tasking Dia and Tarte with handling these assassins served as good training, but I had something else I wanted to see to as well. This trio of attackers was conspicuously capable. Such adroit groups always kept another person hidden out of sight. While the girls took care of the immediate threat, I would stalk for the unseen one.

The dirt barrier crumbled, and out flew Dia and Tarte.

Two of the three assailants stood before their third, who was already working on another incantation.

Dia and Tarte took a similar formation, with Tarte in the front and Dia in the back.

"Earth Wall!"

Dia cast the spell she'd used to protect the carriage, and mounds of soil formed around her. This time, however, there was a gap in the front.

This was something Dia had conceived to keep herself safe while intoning spells. Using magic as a primary combat method came with the disadvantage of not being able to strengthen yourself with mana while working a spell. That left you defenseless. Even with a vanguard to protect you, there would always be blind spots to the rear and sides. Dia's conjured barricade eliminated that concern.

So long as Tarte didn't slip up, Dia had a safe environment to focus on what she did best. She'd left a gap in front so she could launch her attacks. Had she not trusted Tarte, that kind of strategy would have been impossible.

As for Tarte...

"They're...strong."

She was at a disadvantage, only barely holding off the killers because of the Wind Armor spells she'd activated while in the buggy. The reason for that was simple: She was dueling two opponents at once. Both were clearly skilled swordsmen, and they struck simultaneously.

A spear's biggest boon was its long range, but Tarte couldn't exploit that under these conditions. One of her foes easily moved in close, and without saying anything, he forced Tarte back with his blade.

Tarte's Wind Armor wasn't only for defense—she could boost herself in a direction by releasing a blast of air. Thus, when an enemy drew too close, she could use her magical wind to deflect any slashes she could avoid and speed away to regroup.

Unfortunately, she couldn't keep that up for very long. Wind Armor was powerful but brief. Tarte wasn't quick enough with incantations to invoke it again in the thick of a fight, either. Her defeat was only a matter of time.

The third assailant completed their spell, which turned out to be the same sort of fireball they'd loosed earlier. Perhaps it was the most powerful bit of magic they knew.

How dull, I mused.

"Is that the best they can do? Their mage is nothing special," Dia quipped.

She fired a burning javelin that knocked the incoming fireball out of the sky. The lance then continued forward, piercing the hostile caster.

It was an original fire spell that Dia had created called Flame Spear. Unlike most fire magic, it had excellent puncturing capability. It could be guided midflight, too. Dia had sensed that mage was going to hurl a spell at Tarte, so she'd prepared something to counter.

With the rearguard disposed of, Dia had no need to provide

support and could participate directly in the skirmish. The two assailants with swords, realizing this, began to swing more frantically.

Tarte's Wind Armor dissipated. Its time was up.

One of the killers dashed forward while Tarte was distracted by the other one. Her response was going to be too late. The assassin raised their weapon, looking pleased.

Spears were ineffective without proper space between the user and the target. With his distance and timing, the assailant was undoubtedly confident of his victory. He was mistaken, however. While Tarte used a polearm, it was not the only armament at her disposal.

Three gunshots sounded. Tarte had thrown down her spear, drawn her pistol from the holster strapped to her right thigh, and fired rapidly.

Handguns functioned well at close range, even better than swords did. That pistol shot rounds with twice the force of a Magnum, and its projectiles were strengthened with mana so that they could pierce through flesh. I had designed them to make that possible.

Tarte was following orders well. When a gun with a barrel that short possessed that much force, accurately aiming was impossible. Thus, I'd taught Tarte to use her pistol at close distances, to target her opponent's center of mass rather than vitals, and to always fire three times, regardless of whether she hit the mark or not. And that's precisely what she did.

If you aimed for the middle of the body, you'd likely hit even if you were a little off. Loosing three rounds ensured a kill.

Truthfully, she ended up shooting the assailant in the right shoulder, the left knee, and right through the stomach. She'd gone wide of his center by a significant margin. Had she aimed for the man's head, she probably wouldn't have hit at all. A single strike wouldn't have been lethal. That was why aiming for the middle of the body and pulling the trigger three times was best.

"Lord Lugh's gun protected me... Just one more left!" Tarte exclaimed, and she turned her pistol toward the final assassin.

The last remaining assailant immediately tried to flee. It was a wise choice. Dia and Tarte had bested their two compatriots, so he had no chance of winning alone. Unfortunately for him, the girls weren't foolish enough to allow his escape.

A single gunshot cracked in the night. Compared with Tarte's weapon, it was higher-pitched. A rifle round pierced the retreating man's leg, and he crashed hard to the ground.

"Don't underestimate my sniping."

That was Dia's Gun Strike. Unlike Tarte's handgun, which was intended for close quarters, this spell created a rifle that fired accurately from long distances. Dia had grown accustomed to this spell at a very young age.

Furthermore, she'd used it conjointly with another bit of magic that raised accuracy, enabling her to sharpshoot anything within three hundred meters, give or take a few centimeters of calculation error. She could pinpoint aim for vital points with that level of accuracy, and all she needed was one shot.

Both of the girls had grown a lot. As I'd said, those three killers each rivaled a vice-commander in the Royal Order. But they were no problem for Dia and Tarte.

"Tarte, hurry and restrain him. He's the only one left," Dia called.

"Okay!"

Because of how dangerous these opponents were, disabling

the first two rather than killing them hadn't been an option. We chose not to kill the last one, though, so we could get information out of him. That's why Dia had aimed at his leg instead of his heart.

I'd thought it would take all the girls had to beat those three, but I'd vastly underestimated them. I resolved to praise them for this later.

The girls delivered their victory, and now I had to do my part.

When killing covertly as a team, there was a kind of ironclad rule. It was to station an observer some distance behind those in battle. This watcher's job was to either recover allies or destroy evidence if things went south. Should either of those options prove impossible, then that observer would return to base and report on what had occurred. Our enemies were organized and skilled, which was how I knew they'd have someone watching from a concealed place.

Such a person couldn't be overlooked. The guns and original spells that Dia, Tarte, and I used were all things I didn't want others to know about. There was no way I could let word of them leak.

I'd left Dia and Tarte to fend for themselves so that I could locate the fourth member of the group of assassins trying to kill me. While I'd thought it might be difficult, I got a bit of help from an unlikely source—the third killer. He'd looked in the direction of the observer in a plea for help when he tried to escape.

I crept up from the watcher's blind spot and threw a knife that wouldn't strike any vitals. True to my aim, I pierced the side of their torso.

"Hrngh…" The observer repressed a scream and let out a muffled sound.

I'd laced the knife with a neurotoxin strong enough to render an elephant immobile. They wouldn't be able to move anything from the neck down.

"Relax, I won't kill you," I said from behind them.

The observer looked to be a woman. She had a slender build, but the mana surrounding her rivaled Dia's, which put her capacity at the peak of humanity.

This came as a surprise. Her three allies were significantly weaker. Why was someone with so much power being wasted on watch duty?

"I have a few things I want to ask. Answer honestly, and I won't harm you. But if you don't cooperate, I'll use a more forceful method," I cautioned.

There'd been more than a little off about this attack. We'd come to Milteu in secret and had traveled by running, which should have been difficult to detect. How had we been found?

Considering the elite talent of the assailants, only a major noble could've been behind this. However, it all seemed a bit rash for someone of such high standing.

No matter what it takes, I need to get her to talk.

"All right, first question," I began, but no sooner had the words left my mouth than the woman's skin tore, and a giant snake emerged from inside her body, baring its fangs.

A monster disguised as a human?!

I clicked my tongue as I barely dodged the serpent. Then I

swiftly drew a knife from a hidden pocket and stabbed it. Despite what should have been a mortal wound, it passed by me and made off.

"*NeEd To TeLl EvErYoNe, ThIs OnE DaNgErOuS. dAnGeRoUs,*" the snake hissed as it departed.

I felt a sudden assault of dizziness and fell to my knees. Some of the creature's blood had splashed onto me.

It must have contained a deadly poison. One strong enough to immobilize me even though I'd built up a resistance to toxins from a young age.

Hands shaking, I pulled a gun out of my Leather Crane Bag. Then, unable to rely on my blurred vision, I used wind magic to find the snake and aligned my barrel. Instead of using my shaking hands, I operated the firearm using a spell that controlled magnetism.

I have no choice but to kill it.

I wanted to capture it alive to obtain information, but it was a snake. If I hit it anywhere other than its head, its powerful vitality would allow it to escape. The top priority was not letting it return to report what happened here, so I had to aim for its skull. If I tried to capture it and fail, it was all over.

"Gun Strike!"

I fired a bullet and pierced the serpent's head. Unable to stand after that, I staggered back against a tree.

After washing the poison out with water I had on hand, I used mana to strengthen my self-healing and immune strength. This was the most potent poison I had ever been subjected to. Even making full use of Rapid Recovery, it was going to take a while to heal.

No normal monster held such incredible strength. Once I felt

a bit better, I gathered up all the snake blood I could manage. There were many uses for venom that potent.

After a brief rest, I returned to the girls.

"Ah, there you are. What took you so long, Lugh?" Dia inquired.

"Sorry about that. I came across more trouble than I expected. You two did great. Well done capturing one of them alive." I looked at the captured man. He was bound with rope, and Dia and Tarte had stopped his bleeding.

Wait a second...

"Why is he dead?" I asked.

Dia did inflict a severe wound with Gun Strike, but the assassin should have survived if the bleeding had been stopped right away.

"I'm so sorry, my lord! We treated him immediately, but he still perished. We lost a valuable source of information," Tarte said, bowing her head vigorously.

I examined the corpse. "You have nothing to be sorry for. The cause of death was poison. They'd planned to commit suicide upon capture."

There was something else bothering me, but I kept that a secret from Dia and Tarte. The composition of the toxin that killed this man was the same as what was in that giant snake's blood. That meant they actually were working with that monster.

Also, he didn't commit suicide after being detained. From what I could tell, he'd been made to drink an altered version of the poison that had a delayed effect. No matter how this battle went, these assailants were going to die. They'd been disposable from the start.

Dia furrowed her brow. "Hold on. This person is a noble. From a really good family, too. I've never heard of someone in so high a standing dirtying their hands directly like this."

I understood why she was surprised. This man's large mana capacity was the kind of thing found only in the greatest families. The crest on his armor was that of House Auraina, a count's house. They were a major noble clan well out of House Tuatha Dé's league.

Someone that important was used for a job that required ingesting lethal poison? Just what is going on here?

"...His armor and family insignia belong to House Auraina. I also recognize him. This is Count Auraina himself. What would move him to do this kind of thing?" I wondered.

"Really?! What was he doing here? He was an idiot, though. Even after going so far as to commit suicide not to reveal anything, he still used equipment with his crest on it," remarked Dia.

That definitely didn't add up. I would have recognized Count Auraina even without the armor, but it was still careless. Usually, an assassin would want to conceal any affiliation.

Perhaps that's not the case this time, though...

"There's probably some piece of information more important to them than whatever noble houses were involved, and that's what they wanted to hide," I stated.

From the very beginning, this attack had been bizarre. Knowing we were in Milteu, using a noble as a disposable pawn, cooperating with a monster—none of it added up.

Then I was struck by an idea. Maybe their goal was to conceal the true mastermind behind all of this? If someone like Count

Auraina was a mere tool, then it was natural to assume something bigger was going on.

One possibility was a demon lurking in the center of noble society, manipulating many more nobles beyond just Count Auraina. The monster I killed was likely assigned to keep an eye on the manipulated aristocrats. If I thought about it that way, things began to make sense. What's more, the one who took the observer role in an assassination attempt was usually of higher rank. In this case, the monster outstripped the humans.

Did the demon know my location because it had already wedged its way into the center of noble society? I thought this an attack by aristocrats born out of jealousy, but what if it was set in motion by a demon who saw me as dangerous? If that hypothesis was correct, then things were dire.

"Dia, Tarte, I have a question. If demons could wear people's skin, infiltrate society, and turn nobles into their puppets, what do you think would happen to this country?"

"What are you saying? That's impossible," replied Dia.

"But if it did happen, the Alvanian Kingdom would be finished," said Tarte.

I wanted to believe it was impossible, too. But given the circumstances, it seemed feasible. The sight of the giant snake biting through that woman's skin and emerging from her body flashed before my eyes again.

"...Anyway, let's go home. My attempt to capture these assailants failed. Dia, burn all the corpses so that we don't leave behind any evidence of what happened here," I instructed.

"Do you really want to do that? We have clear evidence we were attacked by Count Auraina's house. We can get them to pay compensation," she said.

"That could just stir up the hornet's nest. Let's pretend this never happened."

"All right, I'll do it, then."

I watched Dia get to work. From here on, I would need to be warier of the central government. Natural You's information network would need to look into that organization.

If I could confirm that a demon was among the lawmakers of this nation, assassinating it needed to be my top priority. It would pay for thinking they could do as they liked with my country. Eliminating malignant presences was the long-held mission of House Tuatha Dé.

Chapter 13 | The Assassin Develops Something

After returning to Tuatha Dé, I spent several days in my workshop, preparing the drug with the mushrooms I'd received from Maha.

The substance was primarily a narcotic, and taking it came with the risk of becoming dependent on it. However, it would give me superhuman levels of concentration for a short period. The world would appear to move in slow motion.

My design was based on the drugs that athletes in my previous world used, though my version was more effective. I used mana to nourish and cultivate the core ingredients.

"I don't really want to rely on this kind of thing."

Its power was temporary and would be nothing more than a boost to help me get through certain situations. Taking it was going to harm my body, but there were things I'd never be able to do without this chemical.

The mushrooms were incredibly intoxicating, though that was to be expected of something used in ceremonies to commune with gods. I introduced some additives to increase that effect to its utmost limit.

When it was all complete, I poured my finished liquid into a syringe. Orally taking this wouldn't give me the full effects.

"This is the first time I've used it on myself, but I'm sure it'll be fine."

I'd already tested my creation on the death row prisoners being held underground in Tuatha Dé, so I knew it was safe. I pushed the needle into my neck and injected the liquid drug.

My head became strangely cold, my vision expanded, and everything around me slowed.

This world felt good, and I believed myself capable of everything.

As a test, I tried using one of the skills I'd obtained from My Loyal Knights, an S-Rank one called Multi-Chant. It allowed you to perform multiple incantations at once. While not very flashy, it was supremely useful.

With my mind expanded as it was, I now understood the skill more deeply. I wasn't simply using it. I was diving into the core of its makeup and forcing it to evolve.

The result was a new side of Multi-Chant. I could now quickly perform incantations without the need to say them out loud.

That's right, Multi-Chant didn't give you two mouths. It used mana to perform a simulated second incantation. That other spell was cast by a pseudo-body that wasn't limited by how fast the human mouth could speak.

Suddenly, I had access to a new skill called Quick Chant. Undoubtedly, it would be even greater than Multi-Chant.

"So this is what lurks in the depths of a skill."

I'd found this ability hidden within Multi-Chant. Other skills had to have concealed sides to them as well. Just thinking about it got me excited.

And right now, the one I'm most interested in is...

"My Loyal Knights. Strengthening Dia and Tarte is my top priority."

Dia and Tarte were strong, so much so that the knights in this kingdom weren't a match for them. However, they were helpless against opponents like demons, which surpassed what humanity was capable of. I needed to raise their combat capabilities. That was why I'd wanted to use My Loyal Knights on them.

"...The effect of the drug expired. That's as much as I can do today."

Immediately, I felt nauseous and weary. My limbs may as well have been boulders.

I looked at a clock. The effect lasted thirteen minutes and twenty seconds. I made a note of that rough estimate for the future. Losing the power of the drug at an inopportune moment in battle meant death.

"Seems like the fatigue from using it only lasts a minute, but I shouldn't allow myself to use this successively."

Rapid Recovery helped me return to normal, but that only went for things like exhaustion. It couldn't be used to combat dependence, the other side effect of the drug. Addiction occurred when a strong sense of pleasure was etched into the brain. The only thing you could do to prevent that was wait long enough between uses of the drug. If I became dependent, there'd be no breaking free.

Repeated doses would cause my body to build a tolerance, which lessened and shortened the potency. I would have to use this chemical carefully.

"I suppose I can only inject myself once per day."

If that was true, then I wanted to give myself three days between uses, just to be sure. I was itching to test my other skills, but I needed to restrain myself. This drug really was a secret weapon—the kind only employed as a last resort. I'd have to take care never to inject it recklessly.

With my first test a success, it was time to prepare for the main event.

After waiting a few days to prevent myself from becoming addicted, I summoned Dia and Tarte to the garden. I'd already decided what skill I was going to try next.

"Today, I am giving both of you power using the skill I obtained from the hero, My Loyal Knights."

"Um, does 'give' mean it will make you weaker, my lord?" asked Tarte.

"No, that's not how it works. The user's abilities are copied, meaning I will remain just as strong. So there's nothing to worry about," I replied.

It wasn't an S-Rank skill for nothing.

"I'm excited about this. You and Epona can't even be called human anymore. I've never felt like I had any chance of catching up," Dia remarked.

"I agree. I have been doing my best to catch up, but they're both so far ahead... With this gift, I will definitely be of use to you, Lord Lugh!"

The girls were both looking at me with hopeful eyes.

"This skill does have some flaws, though. If you either lose a battle with something important on the line or disobey one of my orders, you will lose your qualification as one of my knights, and this power will vanish. So make sure you're prepared for this. From here on, you will never be able to lose again."

"Hmm, I'm not confident about that part," admitted Tarte.

"The best thing to do would be to avoid battles you know you can't win, but that won't always be possible. When you do have to fight, you'll simply need to do your best and ensure victory."

"I don't think we really need to worry about that. It won't be an issue as long as assassinations don't turn into brawls," said Dia.

"That's true," I agreed.

We were assassins, not soldiers. We killed our targets before they were even aware of our presence. Letting it become a proper skirmish was already a failure.

Dia brought a hand to her chin. "I'm more worried about the second part, actually. We'll never be able to disobey an order from you. You're not going to make us do anything lewd, are you? You are a man, after all."

"Wha—? U-um, that would make me happy, but I will need to prepare myself first...," mumbled Tarte.

"I'm obviously not going to do that," I hastily assured them.

I could count on these two even without issuing them any commands. That's how much they loved me.

After clearing my throat, I declared, "I'm going to go ahead and use the skill now."

"Um, would it be all right to wait until I got a little stronger? I'd feel better about this if I was already strong enough not to lose to anybody," Tarte said.

"If that's what you're waiting for, you'll never be satisfied. Relax, you're plenty strong already," I replied.

Tarte hadn't been born with natural talent. She'd earned her strength through hard work and lots of experience. It was something to be proud of.

"What about me?" Dia inquired, perhaps hoping to be complimented, too.

"You're practically unbeatable in a battle of magic. I guarantee you'll be fine."

I didn't know of any mages more talented than Dia. Even now, she outranked me when it came to spellcasting.

"Okay, then can you use it on me first? Tarte was the first to get the eyes."

"That's fine with me. Here we go."

I filled the syringe with the drug I'd used the other day and pressed it into my neck. The other day, I'd decided on a name for this chemical: Dian Cecht. It took effect, and my head became cold and clear.

"My Loyal Knights."

I activated the skill. Usually, it boosted one's physical capabilities and awarded them random skills. However, in my current state, I could reach into the depths of My Loyal Knights and have it do something else.

Now I understand. I comprehended the true nature of what was flowing from me into Dia. With that awareness came the ability to alter the flow. I used that to give Dia the best skills for her among those I had and those I'd received from Epona.

Dia's natural proficiency and these new abilities would make her a mage without equal. I could only imagine what she would truly become.

Chapter 14 | The Assassin Is Enchanted

My power surged into Dia.

First, I gave her Rapid Recovery and Limitless Growth. They were the S-Rank and B-Rank skills I'd chosen during my reincarnation. They would allow Dia to overcome the confines of the average human.

Giving her the ability to increase her mana capacity was especially important. The notion of her possessing a mana capacity on par with mine was infinitely reassuring. She'd be able to use spells that previously demanded too much mana for her, and her capability to fight for extended periods would grow tremendously, too.

I could only give her two more skills. For her third, I selected Multi-Chant. Being able to cast more spells was an obvious boon. Quick Chant, which becomes usable after exploring the depths of Multi-Chant, was handy as well.

The final skill I gave to Dia was Possibility Egg. It could become any other B-Rank to S-Rank skill based on how the wielder lived their life. With luck, it would become something she could employ to great effect.

It was clear to me after giving her Possibility Egg that Dia's vessel was filled to capacity. She couldn't receive any more skills, so the process was complete.

Dia wrapped her arms around herself and collapsed.

"Amazing, I feel Lugh's body heat coursing through me."

Her cheeks flushed, and she sighed heavily. Something about this felt suggestive.

"You have now become my knight, Dia. You have gained the skills Rapid Recovery, Limitless Growth, Multi-Chant, and Possibility Egg. Take this as a congratulatory gift." I held out a small bag.

"Hmm, what's this?"

"It's a bunch of Fahr Stones."

"I can see that now!"

"That is the secret behind my mana capacity. Mana capacity and rapid mana discharge increase the more you use your magical power. From now on, your mana will recover at more than one hundred times the rate of a normal person's. I want you to carry this bag around and pour magical energy into the Fahr Stones at all times," I instructed.

"…You've been doing that all this time?"

"Yeah, ever since I was a little kid. Once you get used to it, it's possible to continue doing so even when sleeping. One time, I nearly died by oversleeping and accidentally continuing to fill a Fahr Stone that was at its critical point, almost causing an explosion in my room."

"That's terrifying!" exclaimed Dia.

She wasn't wrong. I'd only awoken in time because the Fahr Stone made a noise signifying that it was going to explode. If I hadn't thrown it out the window immediately, the entire estate would have been blown to smithereens.

"After that incident, I came up with a countermeasure. This one is fine to use while sleeping."

I produced a huge chunk of rock from the Leather Crane Bag.

"Is that a Fahr Stone?! It's bigger than you are!" Dia cried in evident disbelief.

"That's right. You know how I can produce Fahr Stones with magic now? This is a revised version. I made it larger, and its mana capacity has been doubled. There's no danger of it bursting while you're asleep. You can rest easy while using this."

Developing that new kind of Fahr Stone had been quite a difficult journey. I'd only completed work on it a few days ago. With it, I'd no longer have to waste the mana I discharged while unconscious.

"You know, when I was serving as your instructor, you nearly blew up the estate with a regular Fahr Stone," recalled Dia.

"Yeah, I did."

"This is dozens of times bigger than that one, and it can store twice as much mana, so what would happen if it exploded?"

"I wonder. I've been too scared to test it. It could take out the entire domain. Should I have the time, I'll try it out on a deserted island."

There was the uninhabited isle I'd purchased to test Gungnir. The range of the explosion would be too expansive to try anywhere near human settlements.

"I'd be way too scared to sleep with that thing next to me!" Dia actually seemed a little angry. My giant Fahr Stone wasn't without its risks. I'd have to be careful, too.

"Anyway, if you have time, pour some mana into the stone for me," I said.

"Sure, no problem."

Eager to test her new skills, she started pouring magical power into the large rock right away.

"Wow, my mana recovers as soon as I use it. I need to use a

lot of it for spells as powerful as Cannon Strike. I'll have to experiment with Multi-Chant later. Personally, though, I would've rather had Spell Weaver."

"I can just write down formulas for you."

Truthfully, I'd waffled between giving her Possibility Egg or Spell Weaver, but because she didn't need the latter so long as I was around, I went with the former.

"That's it for Dia. You're next, Tarte. Come here."

"Y-yes, my lord. I'm nervous."

"Don't worry. I'll be gentle."

"Okay!"

Tarte's expression hardened, and she squeezed my hand tightly.

"Haaah, haaah... My lord, I...can't take any more...," Tarte managed, panting heavily.

"It's okay. I've already finished."

She looked more disheveled after the ordeal than Dia. Her eyes were damp, and she wobbled on her feet. When she leaned on me, I caught her in my arms and realized her body was abnormally warm.

I gave Tarte Rapid Recovery, Limitless Growth, Beastification, and Possibility Egg.

Beastification was another skill I'd received from Epona. When activated, it transformed the user into a half-beast and bestowed them with overpowering strength and speed, making it an ideal S-Rank skill for someone who specialized in close combat. That matched Tarte perfectly.

"You now have Rapid Recovery, Limitless Growth, Beastification, and Possibility Egg. Like Dia, you should form a habit of pouring mana into Fahr Stones," I explained.

"Yes, my lord. Beastification sounds scary," Tarte answered, now looking a little more stable.

"Maybe, but it's undeniably strong. Go ahead and try it out. You should already have my power."

"O-okay. Ah, sorry, th-that was improper of me," Tarte said, and she hastily separated herself from me.

In her panic, though, she pushed away too hard and fell on her backside. I helped her up.

"Do you understand how to use Beastification?"

"Y-yes, somehow. Hyahhh!" Tarte shouted adorably.

The skill began to transform Tarte into an animal—at least, in a sense. I'd expected her to gain some bestial qualities, but the results were still surprising.

Dia looked at Tarte and burst out laughing. "Ah-ha-ha-ha-ha! Tarte, what is that supposed to be? I thought you'd be down on all fours and roaring at us."

"So this is Beastification…I guess," I commented.

"U-um, what happened? My bottom and head feel a little heavy…"

I produced a mirror from my Leather Crane Bag and passed it to Tarte. Immediately, she flushed red, and tears formed in the corners of her eyes.

"Wha—?! Did something go wrong?!" she shrieked.

"No, this suits you really well," I answered.

"You look so cute!" added Dia.

Usually, the user's muscles swelled, and they'd grow fangs and fur and display animalistic traits.

But in Tarte's case...

"I only grew fox ears and a tail!"

That's right. She now sported red fox ears tipped with black fur and a fluffy tail that ended in white hair.

The big fluffy tail had pushed down her underwear and lifted up her skirt, but she was too distracted to notice.

I'll have to make clothes that compensate for the new appendage later. I'm fine with this view myself, but I don't want anyone else seeing her like this.

"I think you look lovely. This look really suits you!" Dia complimented.

Tarte remained unconvinced. "Aww, I'm not sure about this."

"You seem to have activated Beastification successfully, so how about testing your new power?" I suggested.

"Yes, my lord. My hearing has improved a lot. I can sense the presence of other living things more strongly than before, and my nose is more sensitive as well."

"All characteristics of foxes. Next, try jumping gently."

"Okay!"

Tarte leaped several meters.

"Huuuuh? Why did I go this far?"

She managed to land neatly despite her panic, making almost no sound as she did so. Beasts often killed by taking advantage of their soft and springy joints.

Tarte's physical abilities had clearly increased substantially. Foxes were naturally strong jumpers. Her endurance and speed had likely been bolstered, too.

The effects of Beastification differed based on the animal the transformation was based on. Foxes lacked brawn, but Tarte's swiftness, leg strength, leaping ability, flexibility, sense of hearing and smell, and perception were all greater than they had been. These traits were perfect for Tarte's fighting style.

Admittedly, her adorable appearance was also a plus. I wanted to stroke her tail. That could wait until another day, though.

"You two are now my knights. I look forward to your service," I stated.

"Yeah, you can count on me."

"This appearance is a little embarrassing, but I'll do my best."

The ever-reliable Dia and Tarte had instantly become even stronger. Dia could provide powerful support from the rearguard using Multi-Chant while Tarte maintained control on the front lines with her Beastification.

Their mana capacities would only increase with time, too. With any luck, Possibility Egg would give them both yet another jump in might. When we engaged demons, I would be busy forming the field needed to kill them, so Dia and Tarte would have to fight. Any extra power they could get was going to be helpful.

I couldn't afford to slack off, either. I wanted my Possibility Egg to hatch, too, after all.

"?!"

Suddenly, I detected an intense, predatory gaze. I turned to find Tarte looking at me. The sensation was gone now.

"What is it, my lord?" she inquired.

"Don't worry. It's nothing."

Tarte herself seemed unchanged, if a little feverish. My nose caught a sweet scent emanating from somewhere. I felt as though if I lost my focus, I'd be drawn to it like a bee to a flower.

What in the world was that presence I felt?

Chapter 15 | The Assassin Gives Something a Try

Yesterday, I'd succeeded in giving Dia and Tarte their new strength and skills. As such, I decided all of today would be spent practicing with those new powers.

"Ah-ha-ha-ha! Look at this, Lugh. Multi-Chant is incredible!"

With a large grin on her face, Dia used a magic formula. At first glance, it just looked like a regular Gun Strike, but it quickly became something more.

Dia produced iron, transfigured it into the shape of a gun, loaded bullets into it, and set off an explosion within the barrel. Initially, that process had to be performed in steps, which took a decent amount of time. However, Dia now performed the entire process simultaneously, which enabled her to use Gun Strike far swifter than before.

"You continue to impress, Dia. I can't believe you can already execute four incantations at once. It took me a week to get to that point," I said.

Truthfully, she wasn't intoning four spells simultaneously. What she was doing was even more incredible. She finely adjusted the moment she began each of the four incantations so that they all finished at the desired time.

Anything less would have meant not loading the bullets the second the gun was formed or firing them immediately after. Already, Dia had a great handle on this procedure.

"This skill seems perfect for me," she remarked.

"You're probably faster at calculating magic formulas than me," I said in return.

Dia was a genius when it came to magic, though that didn't explain why she was better than me. Since I was a small child, I'd been honing my mind, burdening it to an extreme that would have broken an ordinary person and then healing with Rapid Recovery.

It didn't matter how intelligent Dia was; she shouldn't have been able to surpass my superhuman calculations. Maybe she had a skill that made it possible.

"Have you ever used an appraisal sheet?" I inquired.

"Never. They were impossible to obtain in my country," answered Dia.

"Then let's find one and try it out. We'll do it for you, too, Tarte."

Because of how scarce they were, appraisal sheets weren't an option for most. Those who could make them were closely guarded. The items couldn't be produced without government approval.

Even with my information network and funds from the Balor Company, I couldn't get my hands on an appraisal sheet. I could have bribed a noble with enough sway to get me one, but that was a considerable risk.

Things were different now that I was a Holy Knight, though. My privilege afforded me access to appraisal sheets. I needed to check Dia's and Tarte's skills.

"That's exciting. I probably have skills just like you do, Lugh," said Dia.

"I definitely don't have any," Tarte mumbled dejectedly.

"That's impossible. You were undoubtedly born with something," I responded.

The odds of either possessing an S-Rank skill or even an A-Rank one were slim, but it wouldn't be surprising to discover they had B-Rank or lower ones. Learning what they were could help Dia and Tarte grow even stronger. Once training was done, I had to get to work finding appraisal sheets.

"By the way, how many incantations can you perform simultaneously with Multi-Chant, Dia?" I asked.

"Hmm, six at the most, but they would all have to be simple formulas."

"Wow, that's more than me."

The most I could manage was five. With that many, my control started to waver, though, so my reliable limit was four.

"I figured something out after testing some things. We're not just performing incantations simultaneously. We're converting multiple elements of mana at the same time as well," Dia explained.

"You're probably right. If that wasn't the case, then you wouldn't be able to use the earth spell to create iron and the fire spell to trigger the explosion at the same time," I replied.

"That's actually the part of this I'm the most interested in. Previously, the spells we were able to cast were restricted to a single element. However, this might mean we can create magic that employs multiple elements of mana."

I hadn't even thought about that. This sounded like a promising notion.

"I'll try to come up with some spells that use multiple elements, too. All the possibilities are going to make this more difficult," I said.

"I already have more ideas than I know what to do with. I'm really excited, but I don't know where to begin. The first things that come to mind are a vapor explosion using fire and water or a flame storm using fire and wind. Perhaps I could use earth and fire to make a more efficient version of Gun Strike. We could skip forming the gun and just use an explosion to scatter fragments of iron. That sounds fun!" Dia was practically hopping with excitement.

This was an evolution. We were stepping into wholly unexplored territory and developing a new dimension of magic. Even the things Dia proposed off the top of her head would be beneficial.

"Hmm, I might be able to make that last one right now. It's only a minor change from the formula we've been using, so wait a second."

Dia then pulled out a sheet of paper and a feather pen from her bag, sat down on the ground, and began to scribble on the page hurriedly. Developing spells had basically become her life's work. She knew more rules than me, and her penmanship with the runes was adept. She was possibly the only person who could create a totally new spell off the cuff like this.

"Okay, it's done. Make it into a spell, Lugh."

The Spell Weaver skill was needed to make her creations into spells, so my cooperation was essential.

"I'm fine with chanting it, but this is safe, right?"

"Believe in your girlfriend, Lugh."

After studying the formula, I decided it appeared all right. I began the enchantment. Just like when intoning multiple spells at once with Multi-Chant, two different types of mana, fire and earth, both went through an elemental conversion.

It worked perfectly. I finished the recitation and cast the spell.

"Pellet Shot."

The magic created over one hundred fragments of iron, which were then blasted forward by an explosion.

Leave it to Dia to figure out how to keep them from flying in the wrong direction.

This attack was equivalent to a shotgun with a large diameter. The range was ten meters forward, and it extended to five meters on each side as well.

I'd limited the amount of mana I'd used when casting, but increasing the power would produce more iron fragments and a greater blast force, making for a devastating attack. The formula was short, so the incantation took four seconds to perform.

"This is a good spell. The range is inferior to Gun Strike, but in close quarters, this one is more useful," I said.

"Mages are in danger if anyone gets close to them. I can use this to fend any attackers off," Dia remarked.

With its decent scope and wide area of effect, dodging this spell was nearly impossible. The pellets were small, but each one had plenty of force.

Dia performed the spell as well and smiled with clear satisfaction.

"If you keep developing useful magic like this, it will help us a lot going forward," I stated.

"Hmm-hmm, that's the plan. I want to make something that uses all four elements! Ooh, an amazing idea just popped into my head. I can't wait to try it."

Earth, wind, fire, and water. It was a little difficult to imagine a spell that used all four of those elements. But if Dia said it was going to be amazing, then I could get my hopes up.

After that, Dia and I spent a while discussing spells we could create using multiple elements. Before we knew it, we had fallen deep into conversation over the infinite possibilities this one new concept had opened up.

We eventually reached a good stopping place, and I left Dia and headed to Tarte.

"You're working hard."

"Yes, my lord! I love how light my body feels."

She was practicing with her spear. The recent increase in physical power left her struggling to control her body. While faster and stronger, she was a little clumsy. Still, Tarte had a strong foundation. It wouldn't take long until she acclimated.

The next bit was going to be more difficult, though.

"Tarte, how about trying Beastification? There are a number of things we need to verify, including how long the effect lasts," I said.

Beastification didn't remain active indefinitely. Once willingly triggered, it remained in effect for a limited amount of time.

Effectively utilizing it meant understanding how long it persisted and the conditions for activating it again. I could use the skill, too, so I had a pretty good idea of all that. However, my transformation was based on a different animal. I wanted information accurate to Tarte.

"Yes, um, well, there are a number of problems with it, so I thought it might be better to wait until some other time…," Tarte protested meekly.

"Issues or not, it's a useful skill. Master it, and it will become a deadly weapon," I replied.

"…Understood. I'll do it."

Something about the way Tarte was acting felt off. It appeared as though she was steeling herself. Thinking back, her behavior had been strange ever since she'd used Beastification yesterday.

Tarte activated the skill, and her cute fox ears and fluffy tail appeared.

Yesterday, her tail had pushed down her underwear and lifted her skirt, but that didn't happen this time, thanks to the low-rise underwear I'd prepared. What's more, I'd given her a jacket that covered her skirt, and both had aligned slits for her tail to pop through without causing any problems.

I watched as the appendage smoothly protruded through the apertures without lifting Tarte's hem this time. Yesterday, I'd carefully noted where exactly the tail appeared. That meticulous measurement had paid off.

"I want combat data from you, Tarte. Let's have a light spar— no, let's make a match out of it. We won't know how strong you've become unless you go all out," I decided.

After passing her a wooden spear with cloth wrapped over its tip, I drew my sword.

"Okay! I'm going to devour you, Lord Lugh!"

Tarte's eyes looked different than usual, perhaps due to Beastification. They were usually timid and docile, but now they appeared combative. The glint in her eyes was positively aggressive.

Whenever we fought, she always gave some self-disparaging comment about how she had no chance of beating me. That was not the case this time, however. While Tarte was more confident, it didn't feel right. The girl definitely looked ready to pounce on and eat me, but I thought what she wanted was something a little different.

Regardless, Tarte was serious about trying to best me. A chance to use my full strength to judge how capable she was after Beastification sounded fun.

Chapter 16 | The Assassin Is Defeated

My match with Tarte began. I had a hunch she wouldn't act like her usual timid self, and that turned out to be correct.

Her fighting style was different, too. Typically, she began by studying me. On this occasion, she rushed forward with a forceful one-handed spear thrust, her swiftest and longest-reaching attack.

Tarte was going out of her way to take the initiative. It was an effective maneuver because it came from a range beyond the reach of my sword.

She's fast.

I'd assumed her speed would increase with Beastification, but this surpassed my expectations. I was in a tough spot.

Curiously, Tarte handled herself perfectly, despite Beastification raising her strength and swiftness. Compared with how clumsy she'd looked during training only moments ago, it was shocking.

I just barely managed to deflect Tarte's attack with my sword, but she quickly drew her spear back and started thrusting at me in rapid succession.

Every one of her strikes made good use of distance, always coming at me from a length where I couldn't counterattack.

While quick, the blows all had substantial weight behind them, too. Had Tarte just been using her arms, I would have been able to knock her weapon aside and move in. However, she threw her whole body into every thrust.

Whenever I tried to get near her, she moved back. Every step she took was levelheaded and astute.

I thought I would try to wait for her to run out of breath, but her stamina had increased, too. As I was dealing with her constant pressure, I actually seemed like the one who'd give out first.

My hands went numb. I couldn't afford to take any more of this. My defeat was imminent.

"I've never seen you fight like this, Tarte!"

Still, I refused to allow myself to lose. Since moving in close wasn't an option, I jumped back to escape Tarte's reach. Then I took a moment to collect myself. I needed to do something about the dullness in my hands and my labored breath.

Tarte froze for a moment. In a battle between a spear and a sword, the latter needed to get within striking range. Tarte knew that, and I'd surprised her by going out of my way to distance myself even further. But that hesitation only lasted for a second, and she charged forward.

Hmm. She fights calmly and efficiently, but her movements are predictable. It's foolish to use the same strategy against me twice. I might need to correct that.

I matched her by dashing forward with all my strength.

"Wha—?"

That flustered Tarte. She held out her lance as she ran to add force to her thrust. Yet, if I could get near enough to her, her attack would be effectively meaningless.

Unfortunately, I still wouldn't be able to draw close enough to strike with my sword, but I had a different goal in mind.

The tip of her spear and that of my sword collided, and the former broke.

Swords were shorter than spears, but they were more durable. Also, charging in close to Tarte had weakened the force of her attack, which led to my blade breaking her weapon when they collided.

Tarte looked unsure how to respond to this development. I, on the other hand, was prepared. Seizing upon her moment of hesitation, I took a step forward and delivered an uppercut with my left hand. This move was much swifter than pulling back to slash with a sword.

The impact should have rocked her jaw and caused Tarte to lose consciousness. Yet, it felt astonishingly soft.

Impressive.

I laughed. Tarte had bent her neck the moment my hand collided with her chin, weakening the power of the blow.

My attack should have been guaranteed to connect, but Tarte had avoided it on animalistic reflex. It was unbelievable how strong Beastification had made her.

Tarte's eyes seemed to shine as she bent backward, and before I knew it, I was hunched over in pain from a muted impact. She had driven her knee into my stomach.

"Gah-hah!"

She followed that by striking me with an elbow from above, the force of which caused me to collapse. Tarte straddled me as I lay on the ground and pinned down my shoulders.

"Haah… Haah…" From her position above, she gazed down at me while panting heavily. Her expression resembled a hungry animal that had trapped its prey. Those fox ears that looked so cute before now lent her the countenance of a true carnivore.

"You win, Tarte. I can't believe you beat me. Can you please get off?"

If Tarte had gone for my throat instead of pinning down my shoulders, she could have killed me. This was her victory. It was the first time I'd ever lost to Tarte in a mock battle.

Evidently, I still had more to learn. I'd been foolishly convinced that my uppercut would decide the fight.

Perhaps I've grown a bit complacent. I need to reassess myself, I thought. Allowing yourself to believe that a skirmish was over before confirming your opponent's death was unacceptable as an assassin.

"Lord Luuugh."

The match was over, but Tarte still hadn't released me. On the contrary, she seemed highly excited and increased the pressure on my shoulders.

Initially, I thought her beastly instincts were telling her to keep fighting, but then I realized it was something else. There was no doubt she was acting on impulse, but the look in her eyes didn't seem combative.

As I pondered that, she tore off my clothes. It was an amazing feat, considering they were defensive equipment woven with thread strengthened by mana.

Tarte leaned forward and started rubbing her entire body against mine. Her fluffy fox tail swayed from side to side, occasionally tickling my thighs. It was pleasant, but her incredible strength kept me pinned.

I had thought that her fox-form Beastification would only bolster her legs, but it must have strengthened her arms, too. So much so that she currently overpowered me.

"Haaaah, Lord Luuuugh."

Tarte's body was unbelievably hot, and her scent was causing my head to spin. If this continued, it could affect my behavior.

At last, I understood. The fire in Tarte's eyes wasn't a desire to hunt; it was carnal excitement. I was Tarte's prey, but it was a sexual conquest.

All right, what should I do here?

I looked to the side and saw Dia glaring at me. Unsurprisingly, being assaulted by another girl in front of your girlfriend was not ideal.

Tarte likely wouldn't be too pleased about her first experience being carried out in broad daylight. Unfortunately, she'd lost all reason, and I didn't know what she'd do if I resisted. She could beat me until I stopped moving and then take her time doing as she pleased.

I guess I have no choice. I'll use Beastification, too.

If I did, I'd have the strength necessary to overcome her. There were a few reasons I didn't like that option, but I couldn't afford to hold back.

Meanwhile, Tarte had begun to squirm and was trying to move beyond nuzzling. Her chastity was in danger. I needed to hurry.

However...

"Huh? Wh-wh-what am I—? I-I'm sorry! I didn't intend anything like this! I, um, I..."

As soon as Tarte's fox ears and tail disappeared, her eyes lost their beastly lust, and her face turned so red it seemed like steam was going to come out of her ears. She covered her face with her hands.

"Uh, first of all, pull those clothes back up," I instructed.

"Eek! Y-yes, my lord!"

Looking very unladylike as she sat on top of me, Tarte panicked and tried to stand. Her efforts only resulted in her tumbling and exposing something even more shameful.

Yep, she's back to normal.

She hurriedly straightened herself up and then furiously bowed her head. "I am so sorry. My vision went red, and before I knew it, I was doing that..."

"I know. That's a flaw of Beastification," I said.

Obviously, Tarte wouldn't have attempted something like that in her right state of mind.

"Argh, I'm never going to use this power again."

"Did you initially hesitate because you had a feeling this would happen?"

I'd thought it was because Dia and I wouldn't stop raving about how cute she was.

"U-um, the first time I used Beastification, I got this peculiar feeling when I looked at you, my lord, and that's why I didn't want to use it..."

"I see. Still, you should become able to repress those instincts with training. You probably don't remember, but you beat me. Surely it would be a waste if you didn't master such strength."

Beastification made Tarte very strong. Her physical abilities increased, and she gained the wild intuition of an animal. It also cleared her of hesitation, which directly improved her combat ability.

Tarte's usual consideration of others and lack of confidence often caused her to falter, which was a dangerous thing in the thick of a fight. This skill relieved her of that weakness.

"I will try my best. But if I seem like I'm going to do something weird, please stop me," Tarte implored.

"I promise I will."

This was a painful lesson for me as well. I needed to remain diligent.

Dia then walked up to us. "You know, Lugh, you didn't put up much resistance. Did you, by chance, want Tarte to have her way with you? Is that the kind of thing you enjoy? Hmm."

I thought she would be angry, but judging by her facial expression and body language, it seemed she mainly wanted to tease. Perhaps she was only slightly jealous.

"It would have been dangerous if I had accidentally encouraged her. That's all."

"Oh, really? I understand. You don't have to worry, Lugh. I accept whatever sexual fetish you have," Dia replied.

"You don't believe me, do you?"

"I truly don't mind if you've taken a liking to Tarte's fox ears and tail."

So that's it. Fox Tarte certainly was cute. So much so that I wanted to use her fluffy tail as a pillow.

Doing so while Tarte was so excited could prove dangerous, however. Who knew what she might try while I slept? I'd have to wait until she could handle her transformation better.

After a week, Dia and Tarte both had a handle on their new abilities. I completed my arrangements for obtaining some appraisal sheets. They were scheduled to arrive in five days.

What's more...

"So they've made their move."

Something that appeared to be a demon had surfaced in the

north, and I'd received an order of dispatch. This was going to be my first job as a Holy Knight.

All my preparation for demon slaying was complete. The only thing that remained was to test it.

Should my spell succeed, it could change everything. Being able to kill demons meant I could save the world without assassinating Epona. If more people became capable of fighting demons, Epona would have less riding on her shoulders, decreasing the chance of her plunging the planet into ruin.

This is going to work. It has to.

Chapter 17 | The Assassin Experiments

Dia, Tarte, and I were off to confront the demon that had appeared.

Horse-drawn carriages are so slow, I thought idly. *Maybe next time, I'll try making some kind of primitive automobile. I should be able to manage that. The poor roads would be a problem, though.*

"This is our first job, my lord. I really want it to be a success," Tarte said.

"I feel the same way. We have to prove ourselves to those in the central government who see me as nothing more than a sacrificial lamb. Remember, if the demon-killing field fails, that means we've lost, and you should only concern yourselves with escape."

The universally accepted rule was that only the hero could kill demons. However, I had produced magic that turned that law on its head. It was our only shot at victory, and if it proved unsuccessful, we'd have to flee.

Of course, I wouldn't let that be the end of it. I'd return to my research to figure out where I went awry.

"Ah, that reminds me. While I can only maintain it for thirty seconds, I can produce the field, too," Dia stated.

"Really?" I questioned.

"Hey, why do you doubt me? I'll show you later."

Short though it was, it would be incredible if someone other than me could cast the spell necessary to slay demons. Constructing the field required a lot of mana, which drastically decreased my combat ability.

If I could leave activating the field to Dia, I'd be able to stay in the battle. Assassination might even be possible.

"That's amazing. I had no chance of using it," Tarte responded.

"You're better with martial fighting. We both have different specialties. Being able to do everything as Lugh can isn't normal. Truthfully, I want to fight on the frontlines like you, Tarte, but I'm stuck with these arms no matter how many push-ups I do." Dia flexed her arms. They were skinny and soft. She trained, but her physical makeup made it difficult for her to build muscle. "Also, I did some more research into the demon-killing formula, and I feel like I can send the field flying."

"Flying?" I asked.

Dia mimed a gun with her hands and made a *bang* noise. Adorable.

"Yeah, the way we constructed the spell, the field forms around the caster. But we could compress it so it could be propelled like a bullet. I can reconfigure the formula to make that happen. That would reduce the field's effect time, though. It would likely only last about two seconds for me. You might be able to keep it potent for ten, Lugh."

I couldn't even begin to imagine how she would revise the equation to achieve such a thing. Yet if Dia said she could, then I trusted her.

The reduction of effect time was because instead of using yourself as the origin for the spell, you'd be firing it as a projectile, which relied on instantaneous mana discharge.

"That sounds good. Can you try developing it for me? There

could be many uses for that. It would be great if you could finish it before we arrive."

"I'll do what I can, but don't get your hopes up," Dia responded. Then she spread out some documents and began to work on some calculations.

Despite her telling me not to, I couldn't help but feel excited. I devoted the time we had until arrival to pondering a way to slay a demon in two seconds.

Assassination would have the highest chance of success. The trouble was the lack of information on the target. While the government had provided some documents, they were not especially helpful. I couldn't form a plan of attack with this information alone. There was nothing I could do but study what was available and expect to learn on the fly.

The journey took several days, but we finally arrived at our destination—a town that bordered a neighboring domain. For a provincial settlement, it was large. It was a prosperous center for trade, as well as a popular tourist destination. Many beautiful stone buildings should have lined the street. However...

"This place looks like a jungle," Dia commented.

"I don't see a single person," Tarte added.

The structures were all overgrown with ivy, and the streets had been flooded with trees. Curiously, there didn't seem to be any animal life.

The three of us stood at the entrance to the town, beholding this inauspicious sight.

I looked over the documents again. Apparently, there had

initially only been one tree, and it then spread incredibly quickly and engulfed the whole town.

Those who had fled early on survived, but there was no word from anyone who'd remained. An armed contingent was sent into the settlement to investigate, yet not a single one of them returned.

After that, an attempt was made to clear away the parasitic plants by burning them with fire. That also went poorly. Only the most intense heat burned the trees. Even if they did catch fire, they quickly regenerated any damage. The military operation failed, and not a single soldier involved survived. The report stated the vegetation ate them.

It was then decided that this had to be the work of a demon, and I was sent to deal with things.

"Hey, Lugh. Are we entering the town? If these trees actually ate people, then we'll have enemies all around us," said Dia.

"There's something I need to do before we move in. Get behind me, you two."

When I accepted this job, I'd made sure to confirm one thing: whether I needed to save those swallowed by the trees. The government responded that even if there were survivors, rescuing them was a hopeless endeavor. Thus, I could use whatever method I wished.

Of course, I wanted to help the trapped civilians, but I didn't understand what this forest was, and running headlong into it seemed like a bad idea. For that reason, I needed to perform some experiments from a safe distance.

"You can see it, right, Dia?" I asked. "These plants are all one entity."

"Yeah. They have mana, and they're connected to an unnatural degree. The only thing that explains it is this being one creature."

"I'm thinking the same thing. Let's do some poking. Keep an eye on their mana for me."

My first experiment was to toss some warm meat into the town-turned-forest. There was no response. Next, I sent in a domestic pig I'd purchased on the way here.

"SQUEEEEEEEE!"

When it got close enough to a tree, vines extended from someplace unseen and ensnared the animal. Several branches stabbed into the pig, and it began to shrivel up until only skin and bones remained.

"That's a nasty way to go, but it explains how the people disappeared," I remarked.

"A carnivorous tree... If they're all over the town, then that means everyone has already been eaten," Tarte realized with a gasp. She brought a hand to her mouth.

As Tarte said, with vegetation covering the entire settlement, there couldn't be any survivors. That meant I could go ahead with my next test without concern.

"See anything, Dia?" I questioned. She'd been watching closely, as I'd requested, making use of her Tuatha Dé eyes.

"There was a swell of mana when the pig was consumed. Nutrients are being converted directly into power."

In short, these trees had been released into the city by someone who wanted to stockpile magical energy.

"Okay, my first experiment was a success. I learned two things. On to the next one."

I tossed a barrel full of oil into town. It rolled until it bumped into a bough in the middle of the road. There was no response.

I aimed at the container and shot a fire arrow at it. It burst, releasing the oil inside, which then ignited. This particular substance was even more flammable than the typical variety, capable of producing large pillars of flame.

Like with the pig, branches extended toward the pillar of fire. It was as if they wanted to be torched.

"I knew they had a strong regenerative ability, but this is crazy," I commented.

"It's still just the typical sort of restoration, though. This isn't the absurd ability demons have to reconstitute themselves that you described, Lugh. I see a lot of mana being used up, so these things aren't immortal," Dia replied.

The tips of the branches regrew even as they were smoldering. When the flames finally disappeared, the trees looked as if nothing had happened.

"That's a significant discovery. Now to truly scorch these things," I declared.

I pulled out a Fahr Stone from my pouch. Like the pig and barrel of oil, I'd prepared this for today.

I usually filled Fahr Stones with a set ratio of fire, wind, and earth mana. That way, I could use a large amount of air to increase the explosive force of the flames and scatter fragments of iron upon impact, creating potent bombs.

This Fahr Stone, however, only housed fire and wind mana. I'd prioritized combustion over explosive capability. It could produce an inferno far beyond what oil was capable of, even my modified variety. It was filled with the mana of three hundred ordinary mages, after all.

It only took a bit more magical energy to push the Fahr Stone to its critical point, and then it began to crack. I hurled it into the forest, and a moment later, it released all that stored power.

The crimson flames spread instantly and consumed an entire section of the settlement. The view was like hell itself.

"It's scary but so pretty," said Tarte, staring at the flames in a daze.

When the blaze subsided, not even ashes remained of the trees they consumed. The buildings survived because they were made of stone, though they were now adorned with black scorch marks of the vines that had clung to them.

"So the vegetation isn't part of the demon itself," I said.

"Yeah, they were probably produced by some kind of ability," added Dia.

Initially, I couldn't be sure if the strange greenery *was* the demon. That turned out not to be the case, though. This forest was nothing but a monster possessed of a powerful regenerative factor. Its nature allowed it to grow through grafting, which explained why the same mana flowed through all the plants.

This was both good and bad news. Since this greenery wasn't the demon, it would be far easier to remove it. Unfortunately, that also meant we'd have to search this large town to find the demon.

"Dia, Tarte, we're entering the town. We're going to search for the target," I declared.

"Yes, my lord! But isn't it dangerous?"

"Yeah, you burned quite a large area, but the town is still full of those man-eating trees!"

"Stay close to me, and you'll both be fine."

I strode forward fearlessly while Dia and Tarte followed behind, looking uneasy. Even when we passed the area I'd incinerated, we weren't attacked. The trees didn't so much as flinch.

"My lord, why aren't they attacking us?" Tarte asked.

"You've been using a spell. Does it have something to do with that?" Dia questioned.

"Yes. Remember the experiment I did before we entered the town? Tossing a simple piece of meat toward the trees didn't elicit a reaction. But they did respond to the pig. The trees don't have eyes, so they can't locate prey visually. That leaves vibration, sound, heat, and breathing as the things they could respond to. They didn't notice the meat when it was dropped near them, so we can eliminate vibration and sound. I made sure to warm it, too, and the plants didn't respond to that, either. That only leaves breathing. More specifically, what they sense is the carbon dioxide we exhale."

The purpose of my first experiment had been to test how the vegetation sought out food. The answer was the CO_2 that animals emitted. My theory was substantiated when the tree branches had reached out toward the pillar of fire.

"So you're removing the air around us and sending it up into the sky," Dia deduced.

"That's right. This way, we can move unnoticed."

I was diluting our breath and blowing it upward. My mana recovery outpaced this spell, so maintaining it wasn't an issue. Having to fend off attacks from every direction while searching for the demon would have left us exhausted by the time we finally found our opponent.

There was also a possibility that the plants shared information with the demon. If we wanted the upper hand, we couldn't afford to fight them.

We had to find our enemy before it located us. Fortunately, it seemed like the trump card I'd prepared was going to be very effective.

Chapter 18 | The Assassin Smokes Out the Enemy

We continued through the town, searching for the demon. It, too, was likely scouring the area for the people who'd burned its carnivorous forest.

To remain undetected, I was using a wind spell to send the carbon dioxide we exhaled into the sky, which kept the plants from noticing us. The demon likely shared the monsters' senses, so it was probably usually aware of everything happening in this settlement.

This gave us the upper hand. Regular humans wouldn't have been able to evade being attacked by the trees. Hopefully, this demon was convinced we weren't near the vegetation.

Creating a false sense of security was common for assassination work. If a camera, guards, or an attack dog gave a target enough peace of mind that they felt safe, it only made the killer's job that much easier.

"Lord Lugh, how are we going to find the demon?" Tarte asked.

"I'm probing the entire town using a wind spell. If I prove unable to find it, then I'll smoke it out using something a little less elegant."

The three of us continued to weave around the plants, remaining vigilant of our surroundings as we explored the town. As we went along, I dropped some things here and there.

It took about two hours to pace around the entire settlement. Whether fortunate or not, we didn't so much as catch a glimpse of a demon.

"We're back to where we started. Guess that means it's time for the dirtier method," I stated.

"Does it have something to do with those things you kept dropping?" Dia asked.

"Yes. Those are special Fahr Stones."

I'd scattered them throughout the town as we walked around it. The twenty-two pieces were all specialized for combustion, and I'd positioned them as effectively as possible.

Tarte turned to me with her head cocked to one side. "Um, Lord Lugh. Fahr Stones only blow up if you fill them with mana to their critical point, so just leaving them on the ground wouldn't do anything, right?"

"Typically, yes. These ones are ready for detonation, however. I cast a spell on them that Dia and I developed. It causes the stones to absorb natural mana in the atmosphere. By adjusting the strength of that intake, I control when they reach their maximum capacity. Functionally, they are time bombs. Those twenty-two Fahr Stones are set to explode simultaneously."

"But every one of them has incredible power. How bad is it going to be if that many go off at the same time?" Tarte asked.

"It will burn the entire town to the ground. That's my plan."

Had there been any survivors, I wouldn't have been able to do this. Yet, given how overrun the settlement was, there was no way anyone was still alive. I'd also received permission from the government to take whatever measures I needed to kill the demon. Razing an entire town was fine.

"Lugh, what are you doing this for? Killing demons is

pointless if you don't use Demonkiller. Those tree monsters are definitely irritating and dangerous, but this feels like a waste of Fahr Stones," Dia said.

"It's for harassment. You saw how those plant monsters eat people, convert them into mana, and store it. The demon seized the entire town because it needs a large amount of magical power for something. It's also possible its goal is simply to produce more tree monsters and build up an army. The demon won't take kindly to all its hard work being destroyed. Since we couldn't find it, I'm going to force it out by pissing it off."

As I explained, the three of us ventured back out beyond the limits of the settlement. We'd perish if we were caught in the blast. What's more, it'd be easier to spot the demon from a distant point.

I dug a relatively deep makeshift trench dozens of meters from the nearest carnivorous tree, and we hid within it. Then I pulled out a special telescope that enabled me to see the town even from inside the ditch.

"By my calculation, it will start in one minute," I stated.

While there was some room for error depending on the thickness of the natural ambient mana, the most I'd be off was ten seconds. The Fahr Stones were likely already beginning to crack.

I was destroying an entire town simply to eradicate the army of vegetation and store of mana the demon had built up. Even the most mild-mannered creature in the world would get angry at such a development. A furious target was less likely to make intelligent decisions, so enraging your opponent gave you the upper hand.

"Here we go."

Despite our distance, I could feel the overwhelming and powerful rise in mana.

"Do not lift your heads out of this trench. I've placed a wind barrier over it to keep out the heat and fire, but if you poke beyond it even slightly, you will die," I cautioned.

Even disregarding the flames, this was liable to be a massive explosion, depleting all the oxygen in the area. One breath of that kind of air would spell our demise.

"Y-yes, my lord."

"Got it."

Tarte clung to me out of fear. Upon seeing that, Dia did the same.

A few seconds later, the world became a torrent of swirling crimson. Fire coursed over the trench like water.

An explosion wrought from twenty-two Fahr Stones, the mana of six thousand and six hundred regular mages, painted the world itself red.

The flames spared nothing, consuming as they grew, causing everything in their wake to vanish as if it never existed in the first place.

I'd filled the Fahr Stones with wind mana to supply oxygen, but even that was burned up in an instant. The next moment, the lack of air in the town created a vacuum with waves of such overwhelming force that even the stone buildings crumbled.

It was like a scene out of a nightmare. We would have been blasted away if we hadn't been in the ditch.

Once it all ended, I took a peek outside using my telescope. The girls both still seemed scared of poking their heads out.

"The town is gone," I said.

"...I've never heard of a single mage doing anything like this. You didn't just destroy an entire town; you made it disappear completely," Dia marveled.

An entire town had been wiped off the map entirely. All that remained now was vacant land. This was what could be accomplished with the efficient use of twenty-two Fahr Stones.

"So, Lugh. If you felt like it, could you do the same thing to the royal capital?" asked Dia.

"Yes. All I would have to do is sneak into the capital, place Fahr Stones in the proper locations, and escape before they blew up. It wouldn't even be hard. So don't tell anyone I am capable of this. I'll be considered a dangerous person."

I intended to pin this devastation on the demon. The government did tell me I could do whatever I wanted, but I couldn't be sure how they'd react to knowing I had caused this.

"Yeah, you'd probably be scarier than a demon to those in charge. It's good there was no lookout assigned this time," Dia remarked.

"If there had been, I would have used a different method."

From a politician's perspective, a human who could make an entire town disappear in a matter of hours was only to be feared. So long as the threat of demons remained, I'd be allowed to live, but once they were gone, those in control would want me dead. Should I ever lose my mind, get bought out by a foreign power, or desire to rule the kingdom myself, then Alvan was finished.

Obviously, I wasn't planning on destroying the country, but the mere fact that I could was dangerous. Removing a threat like me before anything happened was just proactive thinking.

The same could be said of Epona once she killed the Demon King, too. If I really wanted to save the world without killing her, then I had to find a way to remove her power. I had discovered a method that allowed other people to kill demons, so it wasn't beyond the realm of possibility.

"I wonder if the demon is still alive," mused Dia.

"It probably did die, but it will revive. All right, let's see how the demon reacts. I'm not sure what to do if it stays in hiding. Perhaps it will go on to try the same thing with the trees in another town. If so, we'll need to keep blowing them up until it loses patience. I'd prefer not to do that, though."

Carefully, I sneaked a glance at things outside the ditch, looking for movement in what used to be the settlement. The game now was finding the enemy before it discovered us. Patience was key.

I only had to wait two or three minutes.

Another blast roared from the center of the former town. Even as far away as we were, Dia, Tarte, and I felt the tremor.

"GAAAAAAHHHHH, HUMAAAAAAAAAAAAAANS! YOU DESTROYED IT! YOU DESTROYED THE FOREST I WORKED SO HARD ONNNNNNNN! I ONLY NEEDED A LITTLE MOOOOOOOOOOOOOOOOOOORE! I'LL KILL YOOOOOOUUUUUUUU!"

The demon was furious, screaming and thrashing about.

He was humanoid in shape but sported a black horn and green carapace reminiscent of a rhinoceros beetle. The massive and sharp carapace on the upper half of his body made him look incredibly aggressive.

I'd expected the demon to resemble a plant because of his connection to the carnivorous forest, but he looked more like a cross between a man and an insect.

He possessed massive defense, strength, and speed. Fighting this creature was going to be annoying.

However, I'd won the first battle already. I found him, and he still had no idea where we were. That made things simpler—all we had to do was kill him.

"Dia, Tarte. On my signal, approach the demon from the front. I'm going to circle around him," I instructed.

"So we're going with that plan."

"I will protect Lady Dia!"

Dia would spread the field needed to kill the demon while Tarte protected her. I was to deliver the killing blow from out of sight. Working as a team gave us the best chance of success.

This was going to be the demon-killing field's first real test. That went for the spell I was going to use to slay him, too. Still, I wasn't worried at all. There was no one the three of us couldn't assassinate. That was how deeply I trusted Tarte and Dia.

Chapter 19 | The Assassin Spectates

"I only needed a little more." I repeated in my mind what the beetle demon had screamed. Whatever he sought required consuming an entire town's worth of people.

No matter what he'd been scheming, it couldn't have been good for humanity. Simply foiling his plot was already a win.

His appearance also confirmed that he was indeed a demon. During the explosion, he had been in the town, yet he didn't have so much as a scratch on him now. No monster, even one with a healing ability, could have survived that.

"Dia, Tarte, we'll use this opportunity to kill him for good."

"Yes, my lord!"

"Yeah, let's do it."

Our opponent had to have been aware that someone had infiltrated the town. The fact that he'd remained in hiding spoke of a more cautious creature. That had gone out the window in his rage, though. If we were going to assassinate him, it had to be now.

Dia and Tarte charged at the demon from the front. Meanwhile, I concealed my presence and sneaked around to a flank. I'd picked out a number of spots beforehand as suitable for sniping and was heading toward one. My intention was to kill the demon with a special attack I'd been saving.

The incantation for the formula was going to take time, however. I wasn't able to use it in combat, even with Quick Chant. Thus, my only option was to assassinate the demon from the shadows.

Dia, Tarte, I'm counting on you.

I had to believe in their strength and focus on my job.

Dia and Tarte ran forward, their hearts full of fear.

Thanks to the Tuatha Dé eyes that Lugh had given them, they could both see mana and were aware of the tremendous power dwelling within the beetle demon.

Challenging such a creature was paramount to suicide. To make matters worse, he was incensed.

"Tarte, you understand what's going to happen, right? No matter what injuries you inflict, he will heal. What we need to do is restrict his movement and buy time," said Dia.

"Yes, I will keep him still and allow you to hit him with Demonkiller," replied the maid.

"Perfect. I can only use the spell twice, so we can't afford to screw up."

The increase in power Dia had received from My Loyal Knights was what made her capable of using Demonkiller. Fortunately, she'd also completed work on the version that enabled the field to be shot as a projectile.

However, it still consumed an absurd amount of mana. Although Dia's mana capacity was steadily increasing thanks to Rapid Recovery and Limitless Growth, the best she could muster was two uses of the spell. Only being allowed one miss was a lot of pressure.

"YOU FILTHY HUMAAAAAAAANS!" cried the beetle demon when he caught sight of the two girls approaching. His roar became a shock wave that knocked Dia and Tarte off the ground. When they landed, Tarte took the lead, and Dia began a composite incantation using Multi-Chant.

It was Cannon Strike, a spell she'd previously been incapable of using.

She formed a giant gun and fired a tungsten bullet from it. This attack had the highest piercing power of any magic Dia was capable of.

The shot was aimed at the demon's right thigh, a point she would not have gone for had she intended to kill the creature. It was the right spot to target for limiting his movements, though.

True to her aim, the projectile pierced the beetle demon's leg. Cannon Strike was powerful enough to penetrate a steel plate, and it managed to break through the demon's carapace and wedge halfway into his limb.

That meant the creature's shell was harder than steel. Dia's and Tarte's faces twitched a little.

"THAT HURRRRRRT, YOU BIIIIIIIIITCH!"

Without holding anything, the demon lifted his arms and brought them down as though throwing something. A piece of his carapace came flying at Dia faster than the speed of sound.

Tarte used her spear, the tip of which was enveloped by wind, to strike the bit of shell and deflect it. It landed behind them with a thunderous sound.

If Tarte had blocked that head-on, she undoubtedly would

have lost her hands. An ordinary person would not have even been able to react in time. Tarte, however, had improved her vision by pouring mana into her Tuatha Dé eyes.

"Once I find an opening, please use Demonkiller as fast as you can. I don't think I will last very long."

"Okay, I won't make you wait."

The two of them nodded at each other.

Tarte put a syringe to her neck and injected the drug Lugh had created to remove the limiter on his brain temporarily. The chemical sharpened her senses and raised her mana discharge for a short time, but it would render her unable to continue fighting after only ten minutes. Despite that, Tarte judged that the demon would crush her immediately if she didn't use it. And that was the correct choice.

Her instantaneous mana discharge increased exponentially, and then she used Beastification, sprouting fox ears and a tail.

"I'll rip Lord Lugh's enemy apart!" she proclaimed, a savage smile twisting her face.

When Tarte used Beastification, her personality grew violent. During training, she'd learned a method to surrender herself to it rather than try to repress it.

Tarte let her instincts take over and charged. The beetle demon thrust an arm forward and shot needles out of it to meet her attack. The maneuver caught her off guard, but her highly sharp senses allowed her just barely to twist her neck and dodge it. She then stabbed her spear at the demon, but her strike bounced lightly off his carapace.

"Oh, was that supposed to hurt?" the demon mocked.

"...Goddamn bug."

Without coming to a stop, Tarte circled around behind him,

hoping to deliver a blow to his back. Unfortunately, the beetle demon easily evaded, moving a fair distance away. Tarte laid on the pressure with many swift attacks but couldn't manage even a scrape.

The demon's body was extremely tough, and his joints had a special coating that the tip of her spear couldn't cut through. The creature's shell was sturdy enough to stop a Cannon Strike shot from tearing clean through. No matter how much Tarte raised her physical strength, she had no chance of puncturing it with a lance. Her speed and rapid flurry of blows still held the demon in check, however.

"You're so slow, you're going to make me yawn, you piece of shit!"

Tarte clearly possessed superior speed. The beetle demon couldn't keep up at all, and the bullet wedged in his leg certainly didn't help. It getting stuck there turned out to be more helpful than if it had pierced through entirely.

This was not to suggest that Tarte had the upper hand—she couldn't land a meaningful blow, after all. To make matters worse, her breath was becoming ragged. She needed to keep moving at this speed to avoid the demon's attacks, but maintaining that pace was draining. If either her legs or her Beastification gave out, she would die.

Unless something changed, the beetle demon would win. He remained unaware of this, however.

"SHIT, SHIT, SHIT, SHIT! YOU'RE SO ANNOYING!"

He struck the ground with a fist, sending countless stones flying in all directions. Tarte moved to dodge, but one struck her stomach, and she fell to her knees. The direct hit had disrupted her meticulously controlled breathing.

The beetle demon walked up to Tarte and raised a fist. "DIIIIIIEEEEEEE!" His arm rocketed downward. There should have been no escape, but the corners of Tarte's mouth curled upward into a grin.

Thanks to her mana–increased defense and the impact-resistant undergarments Lugh had made, she hadn't taken much damage from the blow to her stomach. It was an act.

Her ploy was meant to give her a moment's rest while also buying her time for an incantation. You couldn't cast a spell and strengthen yourself with mana simultaneously. For that reason, Tarte had needed to make the demon think she couldn't move to gain the time she required.

Tarte completed her spell and enveloped herself in electricity. She and the beetle demon then passed each other by. The girl now moved at the speed of lightning.

"AGAGAGAGAGAGAGAGA!"

While Tarte's attacks had done nothing to the demon before, this one made him writhe in agony and collapse.

Her spear still wasn't able to pierce his carapace, but electricity passed through it and reached the demon's insides. The high-voltage current flowed through the beetle demon's body and rendered him immobile.

That was when Tarte hit her limit. Her fox ears and tail disappeared, and she fell to her knees. Pushing her body so excessively with the drug had caused her strength to wane quicker than normal.

"Lady Dia!" Tarte called out, imploring the other girl to act.

This was the only chance Tarte was able to give Dia. She had nothing left in the tank, and the same trick wouldn't work again. Dia had to get this right.

"Demonkiller!"

Dia formed a gun with her hands and fired a blast of mana. Even for her, the spell should have taken longer to prepare. This was because she'd been calmly monitoring Tarte's battle. Confident that Tarte would give her an opening, Dia had started her incantation early.

Had she started the recitation after Tarte had stunned the demon, or if she'd tried to help out by using some different magic, she wouldn't have completed Demonkiller in time. Dia's belief in Tarte had enabled her to focus on her job and seize this opportunity.

Dia's blast of magical power landed. A spherical field emerged upon impact, enveloping the demon.

This was Demonkiller, a spell that nullified the absurd regenerative power demons possessed.

Dia was nervous because this was their first time using it in battle. Yet the stunned look on the beetle demon's face told her it must have been working to some extent.

In her excitement, she nearly glanced toward Lugh, but she restrained herself. No matter how small the possibility, she didn't want to increase the odds of the beetle demon noticing his presence. Tarte was refraining, too, so Dia had to stay strong.

The three of them were a team, and cooperation wasn't born from worrying about each other, but from each person performing their job to perfection. That was a pet saying of Lugh's, and Dia and Tarte believed it.

All Dia could do now was wait.

Tarte had done well creating the opportunity needed, and Dia had seized upon it and successfully cast the projectile version of Demonkiller. Undoubtedly, Lugh would fulfill his duty and assassinate the demon. There was no doubting it.

After all, if Lugh didn't kill the beetle demon within a few seconds, she and Tarte would be in mortal danger. Dia smiled.

Chapter 20 | The Assassin Takes Aim

I started my incantation as soon as I was sure Tarte would be able to hit the demon with her lightning attack, and I was now nearing completion.

Dia, Tarte, you two did great.

That beetle demon was unbelievably strong. If Dia and Tarte had still only been as powerful as the vice-commander of the Royal Order I'd fought at the academy, they would've been ground to dust in less than a minute. But thankfully, they'd grown beyond that level and had successfully rendered the demon immobile. I doubted anyone else could have managed it.

Dia and Tarte had played their parts expertly, and that was precisely why I needed to do the same.

I poured mana into my Tuatha Dé eyes and looked at the beetle demon. I could see a great stream of mana flowing within him. There was also an energy separate from his mana—the force that made demons immortal. It was stored within a red jewel—the demon's core—that resided in the creature's heart.

Usually, the red jewel was immaterial. However, Demonkiller forced it to become solid matter.

I'd stationed myself about two hundred meters away. The farther away you were from your target, the less precise the attack would be, the longer it took to connect, and the less force it had.

All of that was irrelevant, though. The distance was no problem for the new spell I'd created. This situation called for a ranged attack from far enough away that I wouldn't be noticed.

My new magic was the natural evolution of Gun Strike. I'd wanted a spell that would achieve extreme accuracy and force. Until now, I'd counted on Gungnir as my ace in the hole, but it was too unreliable. Not only did it take a while to land, but its vast area of effect limited the situations it could be used in, and aiming it wasn't easy. This new attack overcame all of those hindrances.

Initially, I'd tried creating something superior to Cannon Strike. Unfortunately, even when I'd used the sturdiest alloy I could produce and strengthened the coating with mana, there was a limit on how strong of an explosion the barrel could withstand. It wasn't enough to be the decisive weapon I needed.

I eventually found the answer after electing to use a method other than combustion to accelerate and fire a projectile.

The name of this new spell was...

"Railgun."

I'd fixed a long gun as tall as I was to the ground. I lay down and gently slid my hands over it, loading a bullet. These rounds were made out of an alloy designed explicitly for Railgun. They were the size of rifle ammunition, but each was close to one kilogram in weight.

The lengthy barrel was fixed to a stand long enough to be deserving of the moniker Railgun. The name also reflected how the weapon worked.

There were two bars made out of a special material within the armament, and an electric current began to flow once a bullet was placed between them. This created a magnetic field that was the propulsive force.

The principle behind it wasn't all that difficult, but it was a very sophisticated mechanism. I couldn't magically produce the pieces needed on the fly, so I had to keep them in my Leather Crane Bag. That was one crutch of this attack.

I inserted Fahr Stones into the long gun and finally finished the incantation. Railgun was composite magic that combined three different spells using Multi-Chant. The Fahr Stones were filled with colorless mana.

They then erupted, and the first spell converted the colorless mana that flowed out of them into electricity. Tarte's lightning spell had come about as an offshoot of my design on this. A strong current pulsed through the weapon.

I activated the second spell at nearly the same time. This one quickly cooled the temperature of the barrel, lowering it to almost absolute zero. I did this to reduce the gun's electrical resistance. Strong currents created heat, which distorted the mechanism and could lead to damage.

With the temperature near absolute zero, that wasn't an issue, though. In other words, the cooling magic raised force, increased precision, and removed the problems of resistance.

Finally, I set off the last spell. Railgun loosed projectiles at such speed that they'd burn up instantly if nothing protected them. Windbreak was the answer to that issue, ensuring my shots would reach their target.

I fired the bullet.

Not even my Tuatha Dé eyes could follow it. A hole was instantly torn in the beetle demon's chest.

A split second later, the aftershock tore the creature's entire body to shreds. The shot landed far in the distance and formed a giant crater in the ground.

"Exact and powerful, just as I intended. This will be very useful," I said with a satisfied nod. There was no magic better suited to sniping than this.

When I'd tested Railgun on the deserted island, its initial velocity when fired at full strength had been 5.9 kilometers per second, or seventeen times the speed of sound. The force was 17.4 megajoules.

This superweapon with rifle-sized rounds packed twice as much strength as a tank cannon. Concentrating all of that power into one point boosted the piercing power significantly. With so much kinetic energy contained in an object the size of a bullet, all external elements could be ignored. All you had to account for was calculation error.

The projectile also made impact astonishingly swiftly. It covered two hundred meters in 0.03 seconds, which was fantastic for accuracy. If a shot moved quickly, there was less time for gravity and other outside factors to interfere.

Undoubtedly, Railgun's greatest strength was its precision. It was a dream weapon that would reliably strike where you aimed. I couldn't think of any magic more suited to assassination than this. Although inferior to Gungnir in terms of raw strength, it had many uses.

If I had to think of a drawback, converting the mana from the Fahr Stones into electricity and casting the other two spells demanded all the magical power I could release, and because the magic was difficult to control, I had to devote my full attention to it, leaving me defenseless.

Another weakness was that it couldn't be used without Multi-Chant. Depending on a skill I'd received from My Loyal Knights wasn't ideal.

Even then, being able to shoot with massive force from hundreds of kilometers away was appealing.

I loaded another bullet. There was no way I'd failed to pierce the demon's core. However, if Demonkiller turned out to be flawed, or if my theory about the jewel being the demon's true essence was wrong, then he would recover. So, to play it safe, I wanted to hit him one more time to give Dia and Tarte a chance to escape.

I watched for any signs that the beetle demon was reforming. I held that position for five minutes.

"Guess he's really dead."

A sigh of relief slipped from between my lips. The Demonkiller spell Dia and I had created worked perfectly, and my theory was now proven fact.

Someone besides the hero could kill a demon. It was an inspiring revelation and would play a part in alleviating Epona's burden. This lowered the chances of her turning against humanity.

I got up and started to pack the components of Railgun into my Leather Crane Bag when I quickly stopped, jumped back, and drew a knife.

"Oh my, you noticed me?"

A single woman with snakelike eyes emerged from the woods behind me. She had dark indigo skin and black hair. Her outfit revealed much of her voluptuous body.

From the moment I saw her, I was confident she wasn't human. No person could have so much mana. She had to be a demon.

This was bad. I was alone, and I couldn't use Demonkiller and fight at the same time. Engaging here wasn't an option. I planned to immobilize the woman and then join up with Dia and Tarte. Once we were together, we'd figure out a way to kill her.

"Please be at ease. I don't feel like fighting. I only wish to thank you for slaying that nuisance, Gurt," she stated with a gentle smile.

Despite her expression, it was clear she wasn't going to give me a chance to flee.

"Is Gurt the name of that beetle?"

In most cases, talking with your enemy is a foolish thing to do, but I saw no opportunities to attack. Plus, if your opponent happened to be immortal, chatting was an effective way to buy some extra time.

I could even glean some information from her with a bit of luck. We'd only exchanged a few words, but I was positive this demon knew things I didn't.

"Sure is. By the way, I'm... No, I'll give you my name after we build a deeper relationship. Until then, you can call me Snake. I came here to observe the enemy. I never thought I'd see the day Gurt died. You've done us quite the favor, killing him before he got what he wanted."

"You called him your enemy. Are demons warring with each other?" I questioned.

"It's less a battle and more of a competition."

Now I had even more of a reason to kill Snake. A contest between demons meant they had the ability to communicate with each other and form social groups. There was a risk she could tell others of her kind about Railgun and my other techniques.

I also couldn't ignore the fact that she had some connection to snakes, and I'd recently been attacked by a large serpent monster.

"A competition? For what purpose?"

"That's a secret. Oh dear, I thought you were the hero, but

you're just a human, aren't you? Wow, your ilk can kill us now? Have the rules changed? Or are you an exception?"

"Who can say?"

Yet again, she mentioned something that troubled me. What were these rules she referred to?

If humans not being able to kill demons was a tenet of some sort, then I had to assume someone set that in place. Perhaps that was how demons had become immortal, too.

"Well, it doesn't really matter. How about we make a deal? I won't tell the others how Gurt perished, and I'll keep quiet about there being a human who can kill demons. In return, can you overlook my presence here?"

She immediately understood not only that I felt I needed to take her out, but also the reason why. I didn't have much of a chance of beating Snake in battle right now, and the terms she offered weren't disagreeable. Yet I had no proof I could trust her.

"Aren't those terms a little convenient for you? You don't want to kill me because I'll dispose of your rivals in this competition. Of course you'll keep me a secret. I want more out of this. Specifically, information. Tell me what other kinds of demons there are—names, forms, weaknesses, and the locations of their bases."

The purpose of my line of questioning was twofold. It served to trick her into revealing things while also probing for what I could. If I was right about her motivation, then this demon was trustworthy.

"You're cleverer than I gave you credit for. Heroes are always such mindless brutes, so I thought humans would be the same."

"You're talking about heroes as if they're not human."

"What are you saying? There's no way the hero could be human," Snake replied with a snicker.

What drove her to say such a thing? It didn't seem like she was talking metaphorically about Epona's overwhelming strength. There was something more.

"So, your answer?" I pressed.

"Allow me to ask one more thing first. Answer, and I'll tell you what you wish to know. Was Gurt the first demon you've killed? Before the beetle, did you slay a pig?"

A pig? That sounds like General Orc, the demon that attacked the academy.

"I tried to kill him, but couldn't. I did contribute to his demise, though."

Revealing that was a necessary investment. Snake's mouth curled into a cruel smile.

"Oh, really? I knew it. Well then, we have ourselves a bargain. I promise I'll give you the appropriate information at the right time... I'm turning around, so if you want to attack me, go ahead. But you'd better steel yourself if you do so. I'll have a delightful time with both you and those adorable girls you're so worried about."

"I wasn't planning anything like that."

I was concerned for Dia and Tarte, but I wasn't foolish enough to show weakness.

"So you say, but I can tell otherwise. You three clearly love one another. You're so cute that I just want to eat you up."

I watched Snake walk off. There was a lot she offered, and not all of it was related to demons. She clearly understood many things I didn't.

Once Snake was out of sight, I used a probing spell to check if there were any enemies nearby, then relaxed.

"I don't appreciate being made to participate in a game where I don't even understand the rules."

For a while now, I'd been pondering the idea that I knew too little about this world. I didn't even have a clear understanding of what demons and heroes truly were.

I needed a plan, which in turn demanded a better grasp of the situation. My hope was that Snake could provide me with the same perspective as those who fancied themselves players in this game.

Unfortunately, it was evident that she concealed a lot from me. I had to be cautious around her. Although she acted like she had no idea of my identity, I was sure she'd looked into me.

One thing I was confident of was that the serpent that had attacked on the way back from Milteu was her spawn. Snake's mana resembled that monster's own.

Snake was manipulating nobles into attacking me; she had to know who I was. I'd chosen to keep that quiet, however, as it would've only interfered in our negotiations.

"I wonder how this will all play out."

Regardless, I needed to meet up with Dia and Tarte. They'd both worked very hard, and I had to compliment them on a job well done.

Above all, I wanted to hug them.

Chapter 21 | The Assassin Gives Praise

Now that Snake was gone, I hurried to reunite with Dia and Tarte. Naturally, they rushed over as soon as they caught sight of me.

"Your spell was amazing, Lord Lugh! It was like a beam of light."

"Man, it's annoying that I can't use it even though I helped develop it."

Tarte's eyes shone with admiration, while Dia looked miffed.

Developing Railgun had been a trying process because of the need to cast three spells at once. Dia had worked very hard to make sure everything was just right.

I'd already had the idea for Railgun before I'd received Multi-Chant from My Loyal Knights. Originally, it had used three mages.

Dia would have used fire magic to control the temperature and lower it to absolute zero. Tarte would use wind magic to convert mana into electricity. I would be in charge of reducing air resistance and firing the gun. If the three of us worked together, we could use Railgun without Multi-Chant.

Our practice had led to Tarte using her Electric Shock spell. If I ever lost the powers Epona gave me, we'd have to go back to activating Railgun the old way.

"You'll be able to use it eventually, Dia. Your mana capacity is growing, right?"

"I'm working hard on it every day, but it's frustrating how slowly it increases."

"Well, I got to this point by working at it since I was two years old. It's just something you need to keep at."

Dia was superior to me when it came to her mana control and knowledge of magic formulas. Unfortunately, her mana capacity was too low to use the three spells required for Railgun simultaneously.

"I do understand that, but it doesn't make me feel any better," she grumbled.

"Even if you can't use Railgun, you do have that other option," I reminded.

"That's true, but it's not much better than Cannon Strike."

I was referring to a scaled-down version of Railgun made for Dia. It used Fahr Stones crushed into a powder, reducing the amount of mana needed for conversion. The result was a versatile spell that Dia could use.

While she was correct in saying it wasn't much better than Cannon Strike, the level of force and pinpoint accuracy was still plenty.

"Someday, I will definitely make a spell that only I can use. Something with incredible precision and that requires special processing ability. Then you'll know how frustrating this is, Lugh. It's seriously annoying. Just watch, you'll have this amazing magic staring you right in the face, but you won't be able to use it. Mwa-ha-ha-ha."

"I'm looking forward to it."

If anyone could achieve something like that, it was Dia. It

would have to be something that demanded a high degree of mana control. Dia hated being wasteful. She wouldn't go to the effort of making something troublesome to cast unless it was worth the effort twice over.

"Tarte, how are you feeling? You pushed yourself really hard," I said.

Beastification took a significant toll on the body. Moreover, she'd used Dian Cecht and fought up until her transformation hit its limit. She was acting like things were all right, but she had to be exhausted.

"I-I'm a little tired, but I'm fine." Contrary to Tarte's words, her knees were shaking, and she was covered in sweat. Even standing had to be difficult.

The side effects of the drug were manifesting as well. Rapid Recovery accelerated her recuperation, but it also caused toxins to erupt throughout her body to expunge the drug. It was a painful sensation. There was no way she was only a little tired.

I smiled bitterly and picked Tarte up in my arms. I was taken aback by how incredibly warm she felt.

"Eek! Lord Lugh, why—?"

"Relax, Tarte. I'm going to carry you."

I had our coachmen at a safe distance to ensure they didn't get wrapped up in this. It would be impossible for Tarte to walk that far on her own as she was.

"But I'm your retainer," she protested.

"Don't worry about it. As teammates, it's only natural that we support each other. Or do you find this objectionable?"

"...No, I don't. It actually makes me really happy."

Tarte blushed and looked away out of embarrassment.

"I'm a little jealous. But I'll allow it for today. You had it harder than any of us this time, Tarte," Dia stated, walking beside me.

"That's right. You did great, Tarte," I said.

She'd tackled the most perilous and challenging role expertly. I'd have been unfit as a leader if I didn't tell her how good a job she did.

"N-no, what I did wasn't all that great. Lady Dia is the one who cast Demonkiller, and Lord Lugh actually slew it!"

"Too much humility can sometimes upset other people. Are you saying that Dia and I are both wrong in our evaluation of your performance?" I teased gently. Tarte didn't pick up on that and grew more flustered.

"N-no, I didn't mean that at all...," she hurriedly stammered.

Dia nodded to herself. "Then just accept our praise happily. Say, Lugh. What if you give her some kind of reward?"

"That's a good idea. Is there anything you want, Tarte?" I inquired.

For some reason, that question made her face turn so red that I thought she was going to start whistling with steam.

"U-um, well, can I ask when we are alone?" she managed after a moment.

"Wow, you want to ask him away from my prying ears. Is it something naughty?" needled Dia.

"N-no, it's not!"

"Yeah, I doubt it. You're not nearly that daring a girl."

Dia liked to bully Tarte sometimes. It was her way of showing affection.

Time passed, and we arrived at the carriage. The coachmen had waited at the specified place, just as I'd ordered. Yet something still bothered me.

I'd had the servants wait here so they wouldn't get hurt, but also so they wouldn't see how we fought the demon. It seemed strange that they'd all obeyed when you considered that the central government undoubtedly wanted information on how I went about killing demons.

I could see those in charge assuming I only pretended to fight and then fled. Surely they'd desire some method of confirmation. Why would they trust that I'd done the job when I had no proof?

Regardless of all that, no one had been dispatched to keep an eye on us. Thinking one of the coachmen might have been a spy, I'd been on the lookout the entire time, but I never sensed any of them near the battle. Of course, there was a chance they moved stealthily enough that they evaded detection, but it was difficult to imagine anyone could outmaneuver a Tuatha Dé.

Something was definitely up. If I thought about it logically, this meant the government possessed a method of checking that the demon was dead without having to be directly present.

How would they react when I told them I'd slain the demon? Why would they believe my report?

I'd have to search carefully for the answers to those questions.

Epilogue | The Assassin Gives a Kiss

Our carriage wasn't bound for Tuatha Dé, but the royal capital. I needed to explain what happened with the demon in person.

I'd sent a letter ahead with a carrier pigeon. In it was a recounting of the demon and how I'd defeated it. I had little to hide, so I explained Demonkiller as well, and I wrote about Railgun in vague terms.

I decided to tell them I'd received Demonkiller from a goddess that appeared in my dreams. I outlined the characteristics and appearance of that deity in minute detail, basing her off of the one that sent me to this world. If she was indeed a goddess, there was a high chance legends of her had been passed down through the ages, which would increase the believability of my story.

My hope was that Demonkiller would spread throughout the land, and the notion that it was magic from the gods suited that purpose well. It would entice more people into using it.

That claim also functioned as a kind of bait. If all went to plan, it'd draw out a certain someone.

We stopped in a big town on the way to the capital. While we could have slept in the carriage, the government afforded us the VIP treatment and took care to ensure we were as comfortable as possible.

Dia, Tarte, and I were each given a special room at the best hotel in the town. We ate a delicious meal and then enjoyed a very satisfying bath.

The staff collected the clothes we were wearing so they could be washed, and we borrowed some comfortable loungewear. This establishment's service truly was top-notch.

After eating, we retired to our rooms. The treatment was so lavish that even Tarte, a servant, was given her own chamber.

I heard a knock, and when I said to enter, Tarte walked in. Her comfortable, thin attire reminded me how attractive her body was.

"Lord Lugh, um, good evening."

"Have you decided what reward you're going to ask for?"

"Yes, I came here to tell you."

The sweet fragrance coming off Tarte was making me dizzy.

It was a side effect of Beastification. Tarte remained slightly off for a day after using the skill. Any swelling of sexual excitement caused her control over herself to loosen. She also released a sweet fragrance and something like pheromones that attracted men and sent them into a tizzy.

Simply put, after Tarte used Beastification, she became irresistible to every man around her, which was dangerous.

However, I was the only person she was interested in. That was a source of comfort. I would have had to forbid her from using Beastification if she'd started indiscriminately assaulting men. Tarte was capable enough to drive off an attacker, but things could get dicey if she were the instigator.

The two of us were alone in my room. Dia was over in hers, working on a new spell. Tarte had stated earlier that she wanted to be alone with me when she asked for the reward, so Dia was doing the tactful thing and giving us some space.

Tarte shyly prodded the tips of her index fingers together in front of her chest. Looking at her was making my throat go dry and my heart beat fast. This was bad. At this rate, her fragrance and pheromones were going to do me in.

"Nothing you ask for is going to make me angry, so you don't have to worry. Whenever you're ready," I said.

"O-okay."

What in the world could it be if she's this timid about saying it?

My thoughts were growing hazy. Still, I did my best to wait patiently. I didn't want to scare her. After two or three minutes, Tarte found her courage and spoke up.

"Please kiss me, Lord Lugh! I want to kiss you for real, not just to replenish my mana!" she declared with conviction, her face turning pitifully red as tears welled up in her eyes.

I stared at her blankly. It was quite the letdown. I thought she was going to ask for something bigger.

No, that's wrong, I thought. It took all the courage she had to request this. Tarte wanted a real kiss.

There were times when I'd pressed my lips on hers to restore her magical power, but a proper kiss clearly meant something different to her. Her appeal was a statement of love, and she wanted me to return those feelings.

Tarte was family. That's what I'd always told her. Yet she had always admired me so much, and somewhere along the way, I came to treasure her. Realizing that cleared my mind of the haze brought about by the Beastification side effects.

"Sure, I don't mind," I replied.

I stood up, pulled Tarte into an embrace, and pressed my lips to hers.

Granting Tarte's request went beyond touching our lips

together—it also meant I requited Tarte's feelings. That was too embarrassing to say aloud, though.

"Mmm, mmm."

Tarte kissed me back. She was lovely beyond words and looked cuter than usual. It wasn't from the Beastification pheromones. This was a warm feeling bursting from my heart that I knew was genuine.

Affection welled in my chest, and I was starting to think that we'd go further. However...

"Let's stop there," I decided.

"Thank you bery much," Tarte replied, slurring her speech a little.

She gazed at me with moist eyes. I knew she'd be fine with continuing, and I didn't think Dia would be upset, either.

But for now, stopping where we did was best. Going any further would've been too much for Tarte. She had her own pace, and I wanted to respect that.

"A real kiss... I'm so happy that I could die. Lord Lugh, thank you very much."

"No gratitude is needed. It was a reward, and I was happy to indulge. Still, I'd feel bad if this was all you got. Before we leave tomorrow, let's go to the market. I'll buy you a present."

"B-but the kiss was plenty. You don't need to go that far."

"It's what I want to do. Try to dress up a little for it. You're so cute. Don't let that go to waste."

"...Y-you called me cute..."

Tarte was practically overheating. She gave the funniest reactions.

Tomorrow, we could search for an accessory that'd bring out her beauty even more. For now, though, she needed to rest.

Things promised to get troublesome once we reached the

royal capital. All three of us needed to relax while we could so that we were ready.

As I'd promised Tarte, we all went to the market the next day.

Dia wasted no time, getting to work teasing Tarte right away. Still, she was capable of reading the room and knew not to say anything that'd seriously upset her. The two girls had grown very close.

"So what did you ask of Lugh?"

"Th-that's a secret!"

Tarte began to flush and grin as she remembered what happened yesterday. She looked happy and was likely glad that Dia had asked. After a moment, she whispered that she'd requested a kiss, and Dia smiled and congratulated her.

It was fun seeing them like this.

The shopping forum was bustling with activity. Stalls flanked both sides of the street, and we stopped to look at one that sold accessories. Judging from his wares, the craftsman was skilled and had good taste. Any of these would really accentuate Tarte's charm, and they looked durable to boot.

I talked with the shopkeeper, and he said he was employed at a famous workshop. He wasn't allowed to put his own crafts up for sale in the store yet, so he used his days off to hone his work and practice vending with a stall. That way, he could learn from his customers' reactions, save money, and buy materials to help improve. Considering how passionate he was for his labor, the day when his creations were displayed prominently in the workshop probably wasn't far off.

"Tarte, which of these do you like the best?" I inquired.

"Hmm. I like this hair ornament shaped like a white flower," she replied, pointing to the object she'd set her sights on.

"That's so like you. There are so many fancier items here," Dia remarked.

She was right. There were many baubles with brighter colors, more expensive decorations, and more unique designs. However, Tarte had made up her mind.

"I thought this was pretty and elegant, and I really like it."

I looked again at the hair ornament she'd chosen. It was a lovely thing, made from a white crystal that had been shaped into a blossom. While understated, its craft was undeniably tasteful.

It seemed quite like Tarte herself. She wasn't the sort that liked to dress up, but she had her own brand of cuteness.

"Sir, we're going to get this one," I said.

"Is this a present? Would you like a ribbon on the packaging?"

"No, it's good as is. We're going to use it here."

After paying, I fastened the trinket to Tarte's hair. There was an effortless charm to it that suited her very well.

"Thank you very much. I'll treasure it."

Tarte patted the hair ornament as if showing her affection for it.

"Please do. And Dia, don't sulk."

"I'm not. Tarte worked really hard, so I understand why she got two presents and I'm empty-handed. It doesn't bother me at all that you haven't praised my efforts."

Her body language betrayed her words. She was clearly upset.

"I have a gift for you, too, Dia. I just need some time to prepare it," I assured her.

"Oh, really? That's great! You'd better not forget about it. I'll be angry if you do."

"There's no way it'll slip my mind. I love you, Dia."

I nodded to myself. Dia was going to love what I was preparing. It had taken a little time to gather all the necessary components, however. Before we'd left to deal with the demon, I'd received a message from Maha saying she'd obtained what I needed. Hopefully, Dia's gift would be in Tuatha Dé by the time we returned.

When it was time to depart, the three of us returned to our carriage only to find another one parked next to it. It was larger than ours and sported exquisite craftsmanship by an elite blacksmith. A monster with hardened rhinoceros-like skin and bulging muscles was hitched to it.

Through the Balor Company information network, I'd learned of domains that had successfully domesticated certain monsters, but this was the first I'd seen in person. A single glance was all I required to understand why such a burly creature was necessary. This rhinoceros creature was leagues above a horse in stamina and strength. It'd get you to your destination far sooner.

The door to the ostentatious buggy opened, and a man dressed very much like a noble emerged.

"Sir Holy Knight, well done taking down your first demon. Preparations are already being made in the royal capital to celebrate your accomplishment. A grand feast is going to be held. Please enter Sleipnir, my carriage," the aristocratic man invited with a polite bow.

I recognized him as Marquis Granvallen. He ranked far higher than I did.

He was a rather impressive figure. The man's demeanor alone betrayed how strong he was. His reputation as one of the most skilled fighters in the kingdom was well deserved. Why was a person of such high standing coming all this way for me? And with such a fancy carriage, no less.

Most confusing of all, however, was why the government was celebrating my victory so soon. No one in the royal castle should have accepted my letter at face value. Something unusual was going on.

"Marquis Granvallen, I am deeply grateful. Dia, Tarte, let's go," I stated.

"Yes, my lord."

"This carriage scares me a little."

All right, what exactly am I stepping into here?

If those in charge did believe my missive, was it because they had indeed managed to dispatch an unseen spectator, or was it that they possessed some kind of system that could inform them when demons died?

The mysteries only continued to pile up as I pondered this odd situation. What was gained by sending a special carriage and conveying us to the capital as quickly as possible? Undoubtedly, the mighty Marquis Granvallen was sent to ensure we complied, but we had no reason to refuse.

Things were growing murkier by the second, but my only choice was to push onward through the fog.

There must be something in store for me at the palace. As I considered what it might be, I climbed into the carriage.

"This is getting fun."

From here on, one mistake could mean death. On the other hand, I was inching ever closer to completing the task the goddess had bequeathed to me.

Afterword

Thank you very much for reading Volume 3 of *The World's Finest Assassin Gets Reincarnated in Another World as an Aristocrat*.

I am the author, Rui Tsukiyo.

This third installment starts to reveal some of the story's secrets, and Tarte really gets to shine in a few different ways!

Some new characters appeared as well, making for an exciting story. I hope you enjoyed it.

The fourth book will see a return of characters from the academy, and those introduced in this volume are sure to get involved in things, too.

What's more, it will have a limited-run edition that comes with an audio drama CD! I'm working hard on writing the script for that right now. I hope you're excited to hear it!

Promotion

The first volume of the manga adaptation is currently available! Make sure not to miss out on Hamao Sumeragi's amazing illustrations!

Another one of my series, *The Reincarnated Prince Wants to Slack Off*, is now on sale from GA Bunko! It's the tale of a young man who's reborn and uses knowledge of alchemy from his previous world to bring fortune to a poor country. The premise is similar to this series, and the main character is really cool, so I believe you will enjoy it!

Thanks

Reia, thank you very much for your beautiful illustrations in Volume 3. I am very grateful that you took the time out of your busy schedule to put your heart into these works. Every time I introduce a new character, I look forward to seeing how you'll portray them.

Lead Editor Miyagawa, you have my gratitude for your constant, quick, and honest feedback.

Thank you to the editing team and all involved at Kadokawa Sneaker Bunko. I'd also like to extend my deep gratitude to Lead Designer Takahisa Atsuji and everyone who's read this far!

The World's Finest Assassin Gets Reincarnated in Another World as an Aristocrat, Vol. 3

Congratulations on the release of the third volume!

It was fun drawing so many embarrassed faces.

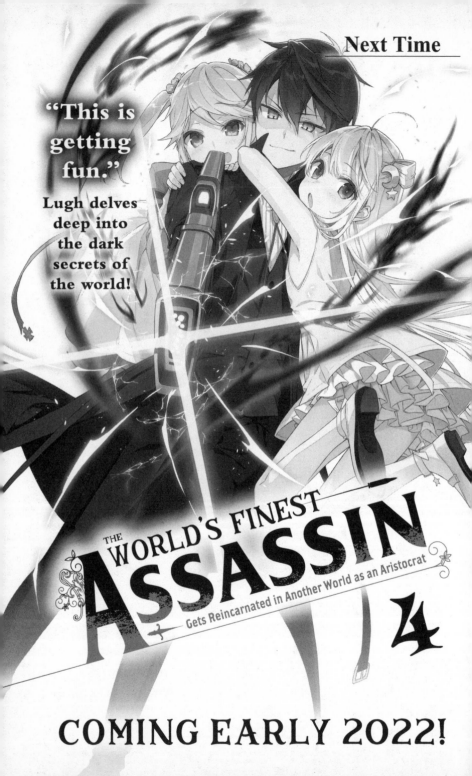

Next Time

"This is getting fun."

Lugh delves deep into the dark secrets of the world!

THE WORLD'S FINEST ASSASSIN

Gets Reincarnated in Another World as an Aristocrat

4

COMING EARLY 2022!